Got To Do Better

By Stephanie L. McKenny

MC² Girls Series Book 2

Got to Do Better

ISBN: 978-0-9705008-0-9

Dedication

I dedicate this book to Michelle Mitchell. My prayer is that you find the greatness that is within you. I also dedicate this book to all the youth of The Love Center Church in Sumter, SC

Chapter 1 - Chastity

I can't believe Jonathan is still trying to get me to have sex with him again. After that scare of almost being pregnant, my guard is up and so are my pants. I'm just not ready for all that baby daddy drama. Somehow he has this wild notion that I'm going to change my mind if he keeps asking.

We're sitting in our third period English class and as usual he's still sending me text messages to my cell phone so that he can try to convince me to say yes. We're supposed to be writing an essay, but writing is definitely not on Jonathan's mind. I hear my cell phone vibrating in my purse and I already know who it is, but I try my best to sneak my cell phone out my purse without Mrs. Smith catching me. We're really not supposed to use our cell phones in class or they will take them from us, which is something I don't get because how can they take something that rightfully belongs to us.

I look at my phone and it's a text from Jonathan. *"Chas, I can't believe you not going to give me another chance."*

He sounded so pitiful. He even added a sad face after the text. I still think Jonathan is cute and I miss being around him because he was the only boyfriend I ever really had since the eighth grade. It's not that easy to just cut him off, but I got to stand my ground. After all, he was about to cut me off and be nothing but friends when he thought I was pregnant. He still claims to this day that he wasn't going to leave me hanging like that, but the way he acted towards me, I don't know how I could draw any other conclusion.

I guess I'm taking too long to respond to his text because he sends another one. I'm not trying to ignore him, but he and I have been over this so many times that I don't know any other way to say no. I know I've got to send him something or else he'll keep sending me these crazy text messages.

"Jonathan, I already told you I just want to be by myself. Remember, you are the one that said let's just be friends. So, I'm taking your advice."

I glance over at him and he's reading the text, but I can tell he's not pleased. He sucks his teeth and then mumbles a few curse words. Another text message comes through on my phone.

"Forget you then. I got plenty of girls who want me. You ain't all that and it wasn't that good anyway."

I read the message and my mouth drops open like I'm at a dentist appointment getting my tooth pulled. He got a lot of nerve sending me some crazy message like that. I must have been all that if he kept me as his girlfriend since we were in the eighth grade. That is so mean for him to say I wasn't good; like he's some sex expert. I didn't know what I was doing anyway and from what I could tell he didn't either. He definitely can forget ever being with me again.

I glance over at Jonathan again and roll my eyes. He turns around and ignores me and I see him sending another text. He can forget it. If he sends another message I'm going to tell him off right in front of everybody in class.

My cell phone doesn't vibrate, but I notice that the girl's phone across from me does. Her name is Shayna Jefferson. She has light brown skin like the color of caramel. She has long black hair, but its weave. Nobody has ever seen her real hair and I'm starting to wonder if she has any. She's one of the big chested girls with a big ole butt. All the boys are chasing after her because she's known to give it up.

She starts laughing at what she's reading from her phone. I saw her texting back. Then I saw Jonathan smiling and looking my way, but from what I can tell he really wasn't looking at me. He started texting on his phone again and then I heard Shayna's phone vibrate again. She reads the text and smiles.

"Yo, Shayna I bet you know how to do it right!" Jonathan yells out in class and then he stares at me.

"You know that. I'll do you right and it will be good too." She yells back across the room and then turns to look at me. She gives me this look as if to say if you don't want him, I'll take him.

I roll my eyes at her too and go back to my writing. Mrs. Smith tells them both to be quiet or they will be kicked out of class.

Even though I'm trying to remain calm, inside I'm slightly boiling. I can't believe Jonathan is trying to get with Shayna right in front of my face while we're in the same class. See, that's why I can't be bothered. As far as I'm concerned he can do what he wants with Shayna Jefferson. I don't care. Knowing her reputation around Midland Central High School, he's liable to catch something he can't wash off.

Chapter 2 - Myra

Slowly, but surely things are beginning to get back to normal between me and my mother. It took her awhile to even begin talking about some of things that took place in our home when Mr. Leroy was living there. She just couldn't believe how he was coming on to me the way that he was.

My mom and I are in the kitchen preparing dinner. Michael is in the living room watching television. Shortly after Mr. Leroy was arrested we told Michael what had been happening. He was truly unaware of what was going on. Michael couldn't believe that Mr. Leroy was doing all that behind his back. It literally shocked him and he thought we were lying when we told him that Mr. Leroy was arrested. It's been a couple of months and now he's starting to settle down with the fact that Mr. Leroy won't be coming back to our house anymore.

"Momma, you need me to mix the cornbread?" I grab the bowl and the box of Jiffy cornbread out the cabinet.

"Yes, Myra, please do that for me because the other food is almost done. The macaroni is just about lightly browned on top the way I like it."

"Hmmm everything smells so good. I can't wait to eat that fried chicken, rice with gravy, mac and cheese and cabbage. I am so hungry and this cornbread is going to set it off."

"Girl, you are so silly. It really looks like a Sunday meal on a Thursday night." My mother laughs as she adds a pinch of salt and pepper to the gravy.

"Momma, I can't help it if you cook so good. Even when I grow up and move out I'm still going to come back and get some of this good food." I pour the cornbread batter that I finished mixing in a bowl into the pan and place it in the oven.

"Yeah, between you and Michael, I probably will be cooking for the rest of my life the way you two eat."

"Oh yeah you better know that especially with Michael because he eats like a grown man now." We both laugh.

Silence fills the room immediately. My mother isn't saying a word. It almost sounds too quiet like she wasn't breathing. Then after a few minutes, I hear her sniffling as if she is crying. I turn away from the kitchen sink. I'm in the middle of finishing up with washing out the bowl filled with cornbread mix.

"Momma, are you crying?" I say as I walk over towards the stove where she is standing.

When I get to her, she turns away from me slightly. "Don't worry about me Myra."

"What's wrong, Momma?" I persisted.

"I just wish I had a man in my life."

I couldn't believe what I was hearing. I often heard First Lady Rice tell us that having a man in your life doesn't define you. She would say that we didn't need a man to make us happy. We had to learn how to love ourselves before we could properly love anybody. Apparently, my mother never got that teaching because she's still got tears in her eyes.

"Momma, First Lady Rice told us girls that we don't......"

My mother cut me off before I could finish. "I don't want to hear what First Lady Rice is telling you girls, Myra. You don't understand. I'm a grown woman and I'm getting older and I don't want to live the rest of my life alone. I need a man." My mother wipes her tears with a paper towel.

"But, you got me and Michael." I continue.

"Myra, I don't want to be by myself. All my life I've had a man in my life. I left from my daddy's house right into a house with your dad. Since me and your dad broke up, I've had someone in my life."

"Well, maybe it's time to take a break and learn to love you. That's what they've been telling us in our teen meetings for girls at school and at our Girls Tea at church." I can't believe I'm having this conversation with my own mother. I almost feel like I'm the parent and she is the teenager. I mean after that craziness with Mr. Leroy you would think she wouldn't want to be with anybody.

I guess I really can't say too much myself because I jumped into a relationship with Xavier Johnson, but that really doesn't count. Xavier had his eye on me for some time way before Larry came into my life, but back then he didn't pursue after me because he saw that I was all caught up in Larry's web.

As we continue cooking, every now and then I can still hear my mother sniffling. She continues to remain quiet until we have everything prepared. We all take a seat at the table and eat our food in silence. Michael and I say a few words while we're eating our delicious meal, but my mother is still very quiet.

I can't believe she is acting this way. The last man in her life brought division between us, but I never would have imagined that the lack of a man in her life would keep us at a distance too.

Chapter 3 – Monica

I'm looking at myself in the mirror in the girls' bathroom at school for the third time. I'm admiring the fact that my weight has come down. My doctor has been pleased with my progress and I think I'm clear of falling into the cycle of experiencing heart disease. I know I still have to be careful because my grandfather died of a heart attack, but at least things are beginning to get better for me.

Another girl passes by me as I'm admiring myself in the mirror. She glances at me for a few seconds.

"You look good, Monica. I know Patrick is glad that you've lost some weight." She walks in the stall before I could respond.

I stared at the stall that she walked into for a few minutes because I was trying to figure out why she said that. Did Patrick not like me at the weight that I am? Has he gone around saying he wished that he didn't date some fat girl? I mean I know I'm not as big as I used to be, but I'm still considered a plus-sized diva. I don't know why Patrick would be so upset by my weight because he is big too, but not fat boy big; he has muscle with it, but he's big because he plays football.

Because I'm curious as to why she said that, I wait for her to come out the bathroom stall to ask her. The thing is I don't even know her name.

As soon as she walks out the bathroom stall and goes to the sink to wash her hands, I ask. "Excuse me, but can I ask you why you said that you know Patrick is glad that I lost weight?"

Before answering my question, she wipes her hands with a paper towel then throws the paper towel in the trash. After her hands are dry, she looks at me.

"Everybody knows that you were real big. I mean everybody on the cheerleading squad was wondering why he wanted a big girl like you instead of getting with Trena Lewis."

"Trena Lewis? Who is Trena Lewis?" I ask. I didn't even address the big girl statement because I was about to pounce on this girl for saying that, but I wanted to know who this Trena Lewis was and what she had going on with Patrick.

"You don't know Trena Lewis? Where have you been? She's the head cheerleader for Midland Central High School and she's president of the junior class."

I look at her like she has two heads because I don't even keep up with the Midland Central High School cheerleaders. First of all, I don't have any interest in looking at those skinny girls jumping up and down, doing back flips and stuff when I can't even bend down and touch my toes on a regular.

"Well, for your information Patrick is real happy with this big girl." I put my hands on my hips and stick my chest out with pride.

She laughs. "Okay, if you say so, but I remember Patrick wanting to be with Trena Lewis right before he started seeing you and she don't look nothing like you."

I was getting offended by what this girl was saying and worried at the same time because I'm wondering if Patrick is as into me as he says. I'm wondering if he's got this Trena Lewis girl

14

on his wish list. I'm wondering if she goes after him will he kick me to the curb.

"As a matter of fact I think she was saying that she was going to see if he still wanted to get with her. And the way I see it, you don't stand a chance if she does go after him."

"Well, the way I see it is if Patrick really wanted to get with her, he would have done so already, but obviously he wanted somebody with some meat on their bones."

"Yeah you might be right about that and you sure got a lot of meat." She walks out the restroom without giving me a chance to say another word.

Every part of my being made me hold back from slapping her down and sitting on her for saying all those comments about my weight. I was trying my best to ignore her fat joke remarks because I wanted to remain focused so I could find out about what Patrick had to do with Trena Lewis. I can't wait until the bell rings for classes to change because Patrick is definitely going to get an ear full.

Chapter 4 – Chandra

The bell just rang. I'm so glad to finally get out of Spanish class. Mrs. Santiago is a native of Spain, but sometimes she goes overboard by speaking in Spanish to us; like we understand what she's saying. Doesn't she realize that this is first year Spanish and not our fourth year of Spanish? Somebody needs to school her quick before she loses our entire class.

I brush past a few students to get out the door and start walking towards my Algebra class. Monica and I have the same Algebra class and we usually meet up in the hallway to walk down together. I'm looking around, but I don't see Monica anywhere in sight.

I look behind me and I see Brian talking to some boy that looks familiar with, but I don't know his name, but I think it's someone that usually gets in trouble. This boy wasn't on the football team and usually Brian hangs with guys from the football team.

As I continue staring at Brian talking to this boy, Brian turns his head and looks my way. He sees me and waves at me. I wave back and I wait for a few minutes to see if he's going to walk my way, but he continues to talk to this boy. That's unusual. Brian would normally come up to me and sneak him a kiss or a hug, but he keeps talking to that boy.

"Girl, what are you staring at?" Monica stands next to me and looks down the hall to see what has me in such a trance.

"I'm looking at Brian talking to that boy."

Monica squint her eyes to look down the hall at Brian. "What is he talking to him for? Ain't that Tyrik Smalls?"

"That's who it is! I was trying to figure out who that was, but I knew it wasn't somebody he usually talks to. I don't know why Brian is talking to him, but you better know I'm going to find out."

"Girl, you know I'll put on my detective's cap and get that info for you immediately."

"It just seems real strange. Usually when he sees me he comes and gives me a hug, but he didn't even come my way even after I waived at him." I peek again down the hall. I knew the bell was about to ring for us to get into class, but Brian wasn't even moving.

"I don't know what's up Chandra. Boys always act strange to me sometimes. I'm starting to wonder about Patrick anyway."

"What's wrong with Patrick? Girl, you better make it quick because you know the bell is about to ring and Ms. Wilson doesn't allow us to even look at each other for a long period of time while we're in class."

"Some girl saw me in the bathroom and said that some girl named, Trena Lewis used to like Patrick and was trying to get with him before we started going together. Then the girl starts saying how she didn't know why Patrick picked me instead of Trena because she wasn't a fat girl."

"Did she call you a fat girl?" My hands are on my hips now and I can tell I'm getting upset because it just kills me how people so freely call Monica names.

18

"Yes, she did, but that's not even my beef because I know I look good now. I want to know if Patrick really wants to be with this girl or with me. The girl in the bathroom told me that Trena was going to try to get with Patrick again."

"What?!!! That is not going down. I'm sure Patrick will clear this up. Have you seen him yet?"

"No, not yet. I guess I'll have to wait until lunch time."

The bell rings so Monica and I slip into class, but before I do I notice that Brian has stopped talking to that boy and is running up the hallway to get to class.

I stand at the door for a minute before closing it for Ms. Wilson. Brian tells me to come out. I nod my head and then I shut the door. I know I've got to get a pass from Ms. Wilson so I go to my seat so she can finish up with taking attendance.

As we're getting settled for class, Ms. Wilson shares what we will be doing for the class time. As soon as she end her last sentence, I ask her for a pass to the bathroom. When I get outside, Brian is still waiting around in the hallway for me.

"Hey Chandra." He hugs me and gives me a quick kiss on my lips.

"Hey, what's up? I saw you talking to Tyrik Smalls."

"Yeah, he was telling me about some stuff he's into." Brian put his arm around my shoulders while we walked down the hallway.

"You know he's up to no good. He always stays in trouble."

"He's not that bad like people think. He's cool."

I stop and look at Brian for a few minutes because for some reason I'm not buying the fact that he's not only talking with Tyrik Smalls, but now he thinks he's cool. Something about it just doesn't add up.

"Okay, if you say so." I roll my eyes.

Brian wraps his arm around my neck gently and pulls me closer to him. "Why you acting like that?" He kisses me again on my lips.

"I don't know something about you talking to Tyrik Smalls just don't seem right to me. All I'm going to say is, don't get caught up in his mess."

"Stop tripping, Chandra. I told you he's cool. Look, I'll see you at lunch time at our regular spot."

"Okay. See you." I give Brian another quick kiss and walk to the restroom. After talking with him I really did have to go.

I hope Brian doesn't think Tyrik Smalls is so cool that he starts dipping and dabbing into some of the things he's into. And Patrick better not dip out on Monica. Boy, I tell you, having a boyfriend at times can be a bit stressful.

Chapter 5 - Monica

The bell just rang and I'm so glad. I almost feel like I've been holding my breath. I couldn't wait for lunch time to get here. I have to get to Patrick to find out about this Trena Lewis and his interest in her. I've never seen her before, but I had a feeling she was better looking than me.

I know I shouldn't think like that, but I'm still trying to break totally free of my own insecurities about the color of my skin and my weight. My friends would probably tell me off if they knew what I was thinking about myself. I know I need to shake these thoughts about me, but I'm just keeping it real. In spite of it all, I'm really proud of how I lost some of my weight. I still have a few pounds to shed, but Patrick never complained and he keeps giving me compliments about how good I've been looking.

All I know is that I got to find Patrick in this lunch crowd. I told Myra, Chandra and Chastity that I would meet up with them later in the cafeteria or after school.

I pass by one of the lunch stations where we can get some food instead of going all the way in the cafeteria and wait on those long lines. It's the same old food; hamburgers, French fries and pizza. I'm so tired of eating this junk and plus I'm supposed to being eating healthy, but these lunch options don't make it easy. I gotta remember to bring my lunch. I get in line and get a hamburger, one percent fat free milk, and an apple.

As I turn around to walk down the hallway, I take a bite of my apple. When I look up I see a familiar person next to a person that I'm not so familiar with. It's Patrick; talking to some light

21

brown skinned girl like the color of caramel, her hair is long and she's thick, not fat thick but fully developed like a grown woman's body. I throw the apple in the trashcan that I was passing. As I get closer, she's giggling and touching Patrick on his face. I'm getting furious and I can feel myself squeezing the life out of the hamburger in my hand.

As I get closer to them, I recognize that she's more beautiful than I thought. She's not black and fat like me. I physically shake my head because I know I shouldn't be thinking like this. I've got to remember what Mrs. Porter and First Lady Rice told me that my black is beautiful. I'm a beautiful girl and I deserve the best.

Patrick's back is turned to me, but this girl is still all up in his face and she notices me coming from behind so she taps him on his shoulder and tells him to turn around. As Patrick turns around and looks at me, his initial facial expression is that of shock. He looks like he just got caught stealing his mother's money.

"Hey Monica......what's up." Patrick's words trail.

"That's what I want to know. What's up?" I look at Patrick dead in his eyes and then I glance over at this girl, who in my opinion, was still standing too close to Patrick for me.

"Who is that?" The girl asks with her face frowned up like I was some stinky trash.

"That's what I need to be asking you since you all up in my boyfriend's face." I was trying to remain clam, but this girl was making it very difficult. Boy, do I need to breathe in and out.

Patrick remains silent as if he lost his tongue, but that girl didn't have any problem talking. She continues and steps right in front of Patrick and stares me up in down right smack in my face.

"For your information my name is Trena Lewis and Patrick should have been my boyfriend if you hadn't got all up in the way.....with your big fat behind."

No she didn't just say that. The milk and the hamburger suddenly releases from out of my hands. Before I know it, I pull my fist back so I can punch the crap out of that girl for allowing her mouth to even say that to me. Patrick grabs my arm before it makes impact on her big lips.

"Hold up, Monica. Calm down." Patrick grabs me around my waist.

My heart is pumping fast and I can feel the tears forming in my eyes because I'm furious. "Calm down; calm down? Did you just hear what she said and you gonna just stand there, Patrick?"

Patrick turns to Trena. "Trena this is my girl and I'm not going to let you disrespect her like that."

"Humph, Patrick, you are fool to pass all this up." Trena took her hand and ran it down the side of her body from her head to her backside.

"Well, I guess I'll be that fool." Patrick says as we stood back-to-back so that I don't start swinging on this Trena Lewis chick.

Trena walks around to me so she can look me in the face and says, "This ain't over."

I'm strongly considering swinging on her again and Patrick too for that matter if he gets in my way. Some people are starting to gather around to see what is going on so Patrick pulls me aside and walks me further down the hallway away from Trena and the crowd.

When we finally get away from the crowd and in a private area on one of the hallways, Patrick tries to get me straight.

"Monica, I can't believe you was about to swing on that girl. Do you want to get kicked out of school?"

"No, I don't want to get kicked out of school, but why were you all up in her face like that?"

"We were just talking."

"It seemed like she wanted to do more than talking. So is it true?"

"Is what true?"

"Did you want to go with her before you got with me, but she turned you down and then you settled for me? Somebody told me that today. They said she was going to try to get with you again so when I saw her with you…."

"Monica you need to stop tripping over this. You're my girl; not Trena Lewis." Patrick came closer to hug me.

I push him back gently. "Yeah, but you didn't answer the question. Did you try to get with her before me?"

Patrick takes a deep breath and then exhales. "Yes, Monica. I tried to ask her out, but she acted like she didn't want to get with me as if I wasn't good enough for her so I stepped."

24

"So what you really wanted was one of those thin, light-browned skinned cheerleaders that can drop it like it's hot, but instead you a got a big ole black girl."

"Monica, you need to stop tripping over the color of your skin. Have you looked at me lately; I'm the same color as you. Like I said, I tried to get with her but she wasn't feeling it."

"Well, it seems like she's feeling it now so go ahead and get that skinny girl if that's what you want."

I start walking away from Patrick before he could respond. As I walk away, I can still hear him calling my name, but I didn't turn back. I'm not stopping. I just keep walking. I wasn't about to let him see me cry and plus if that's what kind of girl he really wants, he can have her. I'm done.

Chapter 6 - Monica

My heart is beating extremely fast as I'm walking around the corner to the other hallway away from Patrick. It feels as though my heart is about to jump out of my shirt. I'm anger, frustrated and upset about what just happened. I can't believe Patrick is playing me like that. If he didn't want to be with me, he should have never approached me. Ugh! I hate boys that try to have their cake and eat it too. I'm not the one to be played with. I can't handle this stress.

And as far as that girl, Trena Lewis is concerned she better watch it. The nerve of her telling me this isn't over. She is right about one thing, it sure isn't over. I can't believe she's actually trying to challenge me about my own boyfriend. All I know is Patrick better do right by me.

I'm walking so fast around that corner that I bump into someone and they're lunch drops out of their hands. I get ready to apologize until I see who it is.

"Monica you need to slow down. Where are you going so fast?" It's Chandra and she looks down at her lunch on the floor and then at me. We both bend down to pick up what is left of her lunch. Pizza sauce splattered, milk carton busted and her apple is rolling around on the floor like it's lost. We get up as much as we can, but we know the cleaning staff would have to get the rest.

"I'm so sorry Chandra. I can buy you something else to eat if you want." I say as I pick up the milk carton and throw it into the trash bin in the hallway.

"Okay, yeah that would be good because I don't have any more money. I spent my last three dollars on what I dropped."

I breathe in and out. I got to get myself together. We remain silent for a minute until we stop at one of the lunch stations in the hallway. I take out my money to buy Chandra another slice of pizza, milk and an orange because they ran out of apples.

"So what had you moving so fast around that corner?"

"It's Patrick."

"What's up with you and Patrick?"

"Girl, I just lost it. This girl in the bathroom told me that her friend Trena Lewis was going to try to get with Patrick. Patrick must have liked her before me, but she turned him down."

"Okay so why are you upset? I'm sure Patrick is not going to fall for her."

"I'm not so sure about that. He said he was interested in her at one time, but because she didn't show any interest to him; he stepped."

"Monica, I really don't think you have anything to worry about."

"But….Chandra." I take a deep breath before starting again. "I saw Patrick talking to Trena and she got smart with me and I started to punch her in her face and then she had the nerve to say it wasn't over."

Chandra put the pizza she was about to take a bite from onto the tray she was holding. "What?"

"Yes." I stand and wait for her to say more.

"I hear what you're saying about Trena and you have a right to be upset, but what I can't get over is the fact that the anointed gospel singer is throwing punches now." Chandra starts laughing.

I smile, but I don't allow myself to laugh because I'm still a little furious. "I know, I know, but she had it coming."

"Well, we're going to have to see how Patrick handles this because the ball is really in his court. You just need to remain calm and don't allow yourself to lose your cool."

"Yeah, I know, but that may be hard if Patrick doesn't do right by me and if Trena Lewis comes up in my face again."

"Let me find out you throwing punches and having fights at Midland Central High School. You know you don't want to get put out of school. Your mom and dad would have a fit!"

"I know, but I just hope the Holy Ghost inside of me keeps me under control." I laugh, but I was definitely serious.

Chandra laughs too. "Girl, you crazy, but I know He will if you let Him. Sometimes you got to do a Woosah." Chandra closes her eyes and breathes in and out like she is in some trance.

Chandra and I continue to talk and share a few laughs. It's a trip how Chandra knows how to calm me down. That's what I really like about Chandra she always seems to help me get back on track with how I feel about myself and she helps me to focus on the right things.

Once I finally calm down, I hear someone yell out something from a few feet away from where we are talking.

"It ain't over, Trick!"

At first, I ignore the comment because I don't know exactly who it's coming from or who they are talking to. So we keep talking, but then the person says it again. Only this time they are standing a little closer to where Chandra and I are standing.

"I know you hear me black girl! It ain't over. I'll get him back don't you worry about that."

It was Trena Lewis and she was talking to me. My heart starts racing fast, my breathing rate increases and I'm about to charge at her like a bull when someone grabs one of my arms. Another person grabs my other arm.

"Monica, don't you do it! Ignore her!" Chandra says in my right ear.

"Monica, she doesn't have a chance of getting me back." Patrick says in my left ear.

Patrick then grabs me closer to him and he and Chandra start walking me away from where Trena is standing. I'm so angry now that tears start trickling down my cheeks. I'm glad they are both with me, but I don't know how much more I can stand with this chick, Trena Lewis. And I'm convinced that if she calls me black girl again in a derogatory way, I'm not so sure I'll be able to remain cool. A woosah is in order. Jesus take the wheel.

Chapter 7 - Myra

I still can't get over the fact that my mother is so upset about not having a man in her life. She's still walking around like she lost a limb or something. It's ridiculous. We're all supposed to be going to church this morning. My mother hasn't been in church for a long time. When Mr. Leroy came into her life she stopped going to church, but she would always drop off me and my brother, Michael so we could go.

Last night, my brother and I finally convinced her to go to church with us. I'm already dressed and sitting downstairs waiting for the two of them. My mother and my brother take the longest in the bathroom and the longest to get dressed. Sometimes I think my brother has girl characteristics because he stays in the bathroom for at least an hour and then it takes him that long to get dressed, brush his teeth and comb his hair. And to top it off, he then has to stand before the mirror to examine how he looks for at least fifteen minutes.

Instead of getting frustrated, I usually do what I'm doing now; sit on the couch and watch television until they both get ready.

"Myra, are you ready yet?" My mother screams from downstairs.

I want to say, what do you think? Instead I say, "Yes, ma'am. I'm dressed and waiting for you two to come downstairs." I hope that makes them both move faster. I then hear my mother yelling at my brother, Michael to get away from the bathroom mirror and get downstairs so we can leave.

About ten minutes later I hear my brother running down the stairs. He stands right in front of me and smiles. I look at him sideways and then I look him up and down. I let out a big sigh because when I look down at his feet, I notice he doesn't have his socks or his shoes on.

"OMG, Michael Anthony Thomas, you mean to tell me that you've been up there all this time and you don't even have your socks or shoes on yet!"

He starts laughing at me. "I couldn't find my socks. I think they all disappeared or either somebody is eating them out of the dryer."

I let out another big sigh. This boy wouldn't know where his head was if it wasn't attached to him. He sees things one way and one way only. Tunnel vision is what he got and he got it bad.

"Come on boy before Mommy gets upset with you."

"I know you can find it Myra because you are the sock police!"

I laugh at his silliness and grab his arm to go with me. He wasn't about to just have me look for these socks by myself. We walk back upstairs to his room and I open his drawers. I search through a few things, but I don't see the socks either.

"Michael I don't see any of your socks. I know Momma and I put a bunch of socks together and we told you to put them in your dresser drawer. What did you do with them?"

Michael has this blank stare on his face. He's acting like he's some zombie and can't hear a word I'm saying. I want to knock him across his head to bring him out of that trance, but instead I ask him again.

"Michael, I don't have time for this. Where did you put the socks we put together?"

After one minute of silence, he finally answers. "I think I played basketball with them." And then he grins.

I let out a deep sigh. I walk away from Michael and go into the garage where he keeps his small little basketball hoop that's attached to the wall. I look on the floor where the basketball hoop area is located and there are a pile of socks all around the garage.

I scream out his name, "Michael!!!!"

He runs downstairs to the garage where I am. I look at him and he looks at me.

"Oh, that's where they are. I told you Sis. You are the sock police!" He laughs, but I don't find it funny at all. He walks over and grabs a pair of socks and puts them on.

By then, my mother is coming downstairs and looks in the garage where we are.

"What are you two doing?"

Michael blurts out before I can say a word, "Myra is the sock police! She found all of my socks."

My mother looks at me and then at Michael. She notices the pile of socks too and starts yelling.

"Boy if you don't hurry up and get your socks and shoes on so we can go! You're about to change my mind about going at

all. Hurry up. And get the rest of those socks out of my garage!"
My mother yells back.

Michael takes off and leaves me standing in the garage.
I'm just hoping that my mother doesn't change her mind about
going to church. Whether she realizes it or not she needs a little
uplifting.

We finally get ourselves together and arrive at church.
We're late for Sunday school, but we're here in time before service
is about to begin. My brother finds his seat with his friends and
my mother and I sit together on the fourth row. As soon as we sit
down, we begin looking at the church program.

The church secretary walks up to the podium and reads the
morning announcements. Shortly after she takes her seat, the choir
starts singing and everyone is clapping their hands, and waving
their hands in the air. As we look around, we notice that some
people caught the spirit and start shouting in some of the isles. I
stand up to clap my hands, but my mother remains in her seat. I'm
enjoying the choir, but I glance at my mom and she's looking
around the church at how the people are clapping their hands,
shouting and yelling out hallelujah and glory!

Once the choir finishes with singing, Pastor Rice gets up
from his seat in the pulpit. He clears his throat and begins
speaking to the congregation.

"Good morning, church. Praise the Lord!"

"Praise Him, Pastor!" Some people respond.

"I have a special request this Sunday. I know it's not normally their Sunday to sing, but I really want to hear these girls sing today. I want to hear from the Anointed MC² Singers. Come on up Myra, Monica, Chastity and Chandra."

Everybody starts clapping and yelling out comments like, "Oh yes, sing girls!" "Praise the Lord!"

Of course, we haven't prepared anything to sing, but it wasn't like we didn't know what to do. Some would say we had a gift to sing. We often hear people say that we make singing look so easy.

I turn around and look among the congregation and see Monica, Chandra and Chastity walking towards the altar in front of the pulpit. I stand up and ask my mother to let me pass by her.

My mother gives me this strange look like I was an alien from another planet. "Where are you going?"

I lean over to whisper in her ear. "I'm going up there to sing."

My mother gives me another strange look as if to say she didn't know what I was going up there for because I couldn't sing. My mother doesn't even have a clue that I actually can sing and I'm actually good at it too. All of us were. She has been so caught up with Mr. Leroy that she didn't even realize how much talent me and my friends actually have.

I cut across her, walk to the altar and stand in front of one of the four microphones they placed out for us. The congregation was cheering us on, but by the puzzled look on my mother's face, I could tell she was still trying to figure out if I can sing.

We start singing an old gospel hymn, I Need Thee. The harmony is so clear. Everyone is standing up and enjoying every bit of it. People are waving their hands in the air, and some are yelling out their usual hallelujah and saying thank you Jesus. As I take another look around the congregation, I even see my mother standing up and her hand went in the air one time. I guess the song was touching her heart as well.

After we sat down, Pastor Rice got up in the pulpit and gave us accolades on what we sang.

"Yes, church we all need the Lord!" He began.

"Yes, sir!" One of the deacons responds.

"The song that the girls sang this morning is right in line with what I want to share today. We all need the Lord, every hour. Some people think they can live without Him, but we need the Lord every day of our lives. Sometimes people go through things in life and they don't know where to turn, but I know someone who is always there when you need Him. He may not come when you want Him, but He's always on time. Can I get a witness?"

"Amen, Pastor!"

"You talking right, Pastor!"

"You see, we think we're alone, but we're not alone at all. God is with us. Not only is He with us, He also makes us complete. A woman doesn't need a man to make her complete, she can be complete in God and find wholeness in Him. For Colossians 2:10 tells us that we are complete in Him. We shouldn't make outside people responsible for making us feel complete or make us feel good about ourselves, we need to know that we're already complete through God."

As Pastor Rice was talking about being complete in God, I could tell he had my mother's undivided attention. She didn't say a word, nor did she look my way. I was hoping that her silence was an indication that she was taking all this in. The thought of her thinking she needed to have a man in her life to be happy was a bit much. I mean after dealing with all the drama we had to go through with her dating Mr. Leroy was enough pain to make somebody not want to be with anybody. I just hope she will give herself time to heal before she gets involved with someone else. I guess time will tell.

Chapter 8 – Chastity

I'm just getting home from church. I already changed my clothes so I'm just chilling on my bed while I'm playing some games on my phone.

Church was good, and I was so glad to see Myra and her mother come to church. She hadn't been in a long time so it was good to see her. We all decided that we would get together later this afternoon to have a little girl talk.

I don't have any real drama to discuss since Jonathan is out of my life. I'm drama free and I'm glad about it. Every now and then, Jonathan still tries to ask me if I'm going to have sex with him again. Every time he asks, I tell him no. I'm not about to go through that drama again. At this point, I'm too afraid to even take the risk of having sex because I might get pregnant for real.

Besides, Jonathan seems to be trying to play me for a fool because even though he keeps asking me for sex, he's got his face all up in Shayna Jefferson's face. The last I heard he was having sex with her. As far as I'm concerned he's dumb and so is she.

He's dumb because Shayna sleeps around and she doesn't use protection when she does. There's no telling what he may end up with. She's dumb, because she doesn't realize that the only thing these guys want is what's between her legs. For some reason, I get this impression that she thinks these boys really want to be with her. Doesn't she realize that in high school, boys don't want a lasting relationship? Doesn't she get it that they just want to see how many girls they can have sex with? Somebody needs to school her quick, but it won't be me.

I turn on the television and I'm flicking through the channels. I put my phone down for a minute because I start looking at Daddy's Girls.

The more I keep watching this movie, the more I can feel myself getting sleepy. I'm really trying my best to stay awake. Oh Lord, I feel myself drifting, but I suddenly jump because I hear my cell phone making this chirping noise to let me know I got a new text message.

I grab my phone and see that it's Jonathan sending me a message.

"Chas, you need to stop holding back on me. We've been with each other too long for you to cut me off like this."

I let out a big sigh because I can't believe Jonathan is still going on about this. He's right; we've been with each other a long time prior to our breakup, but I wasn't about to get trapped up in that again. Especially when he thought I was pregnant and he acted like he didn't know me or want anything to do with me.

I don't even respond. I keep looking at television and then the phone chirps again.

"Chas, why you acting like you don't want nothing to do with me."

"That's because I don't." I respond back to him.

"So you just going to cut me off like that?"

"Yup!"

"Chas, you about to make me do something I really don't want to do."

40

"Jonathan, what are you talking about?" I text back, but I'm slightly frustrated now because I don't know why he keeps bothering me about this. He got Shayna to mess around with. Why does he keep bothering me?

"Are you going to talk to me?"

"Talk to you about what? There is nothing to talk about. Go talk to Shayna!"

"See, why you had to go there?"

"Because you're going there! Get it from her like you said you was so loud in class."

"I only said that to make you mad."

"You still messing with her. Everybody knows it, but I'm not even mad. Go ahead and do you!"

"Chas don't even act like that. I said if you don't talk to me you gonna make me do something I don't want to do.

"Whatever, Jonathan! Bye!"

I push on the power off button on my phone and put it down on my bed. I'm tired of this game now. I mean who does he think he is? He thinks he can just come in and out of my life. Nope. I'm not about to be played twice. It's not going down. I don't know what he was talking about when he said he was going to do something he really didn't want to, but Jonathan Berry will just have to get over Chastity Renee Robertson once and for all.

Chapter 9 - Myra

After church, while we're driving home and when we get home my mother keeps telling me how much she enjoyed hearing me and the girls sing. She didn't realize that I had that much talent. She was blown away to hear how strong a voice Monica had also. Once again she's sharing her thoughts with me about my singing.

"Myra, I had no idea that your voice was so beautiful. How did you manage to keep this from me?"

"I don't know how you didn't know. You don't remember hearing me sing around the house in my room?"

My mother just stood in front of me with a blank stare like she had no clue.

"Yeah, Momma she's always singing in her room. Sometimes I have to knock on my bedroom wall to get her to stop." Michael interjects.

I pop my brother on the head for saying that. I'm only playing with him so he runs off laughing.

"I don't know how I missed that." My mother says while taking a seat on one of the chairs in the kitchen.

"Well, it could be that you were so wrapped up in Mr. Leroy that you didn't even notice me or Michael." I respond.

I could tell that I hit a nerve when I made that comment because my mother jumps right up and gets in my face.

"Listen, little girl, I don't need you to keep reminding me of my past. I know I got a little detached from you and your brother when Leroy was here, but I don't need you to keep slapping me in my face with it." My mother took a deep breath, but she kept her hands on her hips as if there was more she was going to say.

Michael saw the look on my mother's face too so he jumps in the conversation.

"Momma, don't get mad at Myra. It's not her fault. She's telling the truth. When Mr. Leroy was here it was as if we didn't have a mother. I mean, he was cool with me, but the way you started changing wasn't cool at all."

I remain silent and wait to hear my mother's response to Michael. Michael was younger than I was and his feelings are genuine. Even though he and Mr. Leroy got along slightly, Michael wasn't a fool. We were losing our mother to a complete nut case.

"Michael, you need to watch your mouth." That was all my mother could release out of her mouth.

"Mom, we don't mean any harm. We only brought it up because you were trying to figure out why you didn't know I could sing." I walk over to where my mother was sitting and grab her hand.

"We just need you to know that we missed you and we don't want you to be with someone that is going to harm you or us. That just ain't cool."

Michael walks over and stands by our mother too. "Yeah, I don't want anybody to hurt you, me or my sister. And I don't like that drinking either."

I was shocked that Michael went there about the drinking, but I'm glad he did. Our mother drank like a fish in sea water. It got to the point that she was drinking every day at all times of the day. Many of the arguments she and I had were because she was drunk.

"Michael Anthony Thomas! You better stop while you got a chance to still breathe in front of me." My mother snaps back. I get the impression that she wasn't up for hearing all about how that whole situation made us feel.

"Momma, we don't want to get in no argument with you. I guess what we're trying to say is that we missed you, we need you and we don't want anyone to come between us again." I say as calmly as I know how. I didn't want my brother to have to suffer for telling the truth.

"Yeah, that's it. Myra is so smart." Michael places his hand on his forehead and shakes his head. There was a little bit of sarcasm in Michael's voice. I detected it and I guess my mother did too because she starts laughing a little.

She let out a big sigh and says, "Okay, okay I guess I understand what you two are trying to tell me. I guess I didn't realize how much I was losing when I was with him."

My mother looks at me and says, "Myra, can you forgive me for not believing you? I know you tried so many times to tell me that Leroy was no good, but I couldn't see it because I didn't want to be alone."

"I forgive you. I'm just glad it's over."

"Yes, I'm glad it's over too. I just wonder how long I'll have to be single."

"You don't need a boyfriend, Mommy. Not while you got me. I'll be the man of house." Michael says while flexing his muscles as if he was Mr. Universe or something.

My mom laughs uncontrollably for a while. "I hear you Michael. I guess you'll have to be the man of the house until I get a man."

"Momma, remember what Pastor Rice said about being complete. You really don't need a man." I mention again, but I don't think I was convincing my mother at all. I remember the guy my mother was dating before Leroy and he wasn't any good either. I don't know if Michael and I could handle another drama-filled relationship from our mother.

"I heard that preacher Myra, but he got a wife to keep him company."

Oh boy, sounds like it's going to take more than one visit to church to get my mother to see that she didn't need a man in her life to make her complete. I have no clue who she's going to hook up with, I just hope it won't turn our house into a place of drama again. I don't know if I can handle it.

Chapter 10 – Chandra

I've been home from church for a while now, but I've been relaxing since I got in. I know it's almost that time to meet up with my friends so I'm trying to figure out what to wear. After looking through my closet several times, I finally decide to put on my jeans and a purple shirt. Purple is one of my favorite colors because it's a color of royalty. First Lady Rice always told us that. Yup, I'm a queen at heart and can't nobody tell me differently.

I know one thing, Brian Miller better recognize it. He got a queen and he better make sure he continues to do right by me. I definitely don't have no time for no drama. Brian must have me on his mind too because my cell phone is ringing and it's him.

"Hey Brian."

"Hey Chandra. What are you doing?"

"I'm just chilling. Waiting on my friends to call so we can go out to eat."

"Humph. You always hanging with them. You need to be with your man."

I can sense a slight sound of irritation in Brian's voice. He's acting as if he got a problem with me being with my friends. He's never acted this way before.

"What are you talking about Brian? You know me and my friends always do something after church when we have to sing."

"Yeah, well you need to switch it up sometimes. How you expect us to go further in our relationship if you always hanging with them?"

I honestly didn't know where this was going or even why it was even being brought up, but I'm sure soon enough he'll really tell me what's up. I don't know why boys sometimes talk in circles. It's like they expect us to guess what's going on with them. Mind reading is definitely not my forte and I'm not about to begin learning it now.

"Brian, I don't understand what you mean. What's wrong with our relationship? I thought we were good."

"It ain't going be good if we hardly spend time together. We need to do more than what we doing Chandra Mitchell."

Why did he call my whole name? What is up with this brother today? I don't know how to respond so he keeps talking.

"You act like you don't want to do nothing else with me."

"What are you talking about Brian? Do something else, like what?"

He lets out a long sigh before finally answering me.

"Chandra, if you don't get it then I don't think I need to be explaining it to you."

"Brian, I really wish you would stop talking in circles and just tell me what's on your mind." I'm getting frustrated with all this around-the-bush talk. I need him to get to the point and get to it quick.

"Circles? I'm not talking in no circles; you just don't get it do you? You need to spend more time with me so we can do some other things in this relationship. Act like you my girl!"

Now I'm really confused. I thought I was his girl. What in the world is he talking about? What things is he talking about doing? I mean does he want to go to different places on our dates? Does he want to see me more? Does he want me to cut off my friends totally? I wish for one minute I could get inside his head, walk around in it and find out what he is really trying to tell me. I am not a psychic or even a prophetess for that matter.

"Brian, I am your girl. Unless you trying to tell me something different." At this point I'm really tired of this game. He needs to tell me more than all this circle talking. Before this point I thought we were good.

"You are my girl, Chandra, but I want us to get closer."

"Okay."

"You say okay, but do you mean it?"

"Yes, I guess so. I mean I thought we were good."

"What you mean, you guess so? Either you want to get closer or you don't. See, Tyrik was right…."

Before Brian could finish his sentence, I interrupt him because if this whole crazy conversation is because of Tyrik Smalls then I got to give Brian a piece of my mind.

"What does Tyrik have to do with me and you, Brian Miller?" I had to say his full name this time because I was getting fed up with this.

"He doesn't have anything to do with it, but he was sharing some things with me and it all makes sense. We just got to get closer and that means you're going to have to start giving me more

49

than them short little pecks on my lips for kisses. We just got to do more than what we doing."

"Who said we got to do more? And what's wrong with the way we kiss? You never said nothing before. Now that Tyrik is all up in your ear; you got an issue with it?"

"This ain't about Tyrik. It's about us. We kiss like we're in the third grade, Chandra. I want us to kiss with our tongues and do more stuff."

I keep quiet because I'm not so sure where this is going. I could possibly let Brian tongue kiss me, but I don't know what he means about doing more stuff. I'm not about to get naked so he better forget that. It's not going down, not now, not never. I've had enough of this conversation.

"Never mind Chandra, you don't get it. If you don't want none of this, I'm sure someone else will."

Before I could even respond to that nonsense, there was silence on the other end of the phone. He hung up on me. What in the world is wrong with him? As I'm sitting here thinking about the conversation, I know exactly what's wrong with Brian. His name is Tyrik Smalls and I knew he was no good for Brian to be around. I can't wait until we get to school tomorrow. I'm going to have a whole lot to say to Brian Miller and I got a few not-so-nice words for Tyrik, if I see him.

Chapter 11 - Myra

I still can't get over how my mother acted after church. This is so ridiculous. Why does she have to have a man? I really don't think she knows how to pick one that's why she needs Jesus quick. I'm sure He could help her find the right one because if she keeps trying to pick one, it's going to be tough for me and Michael for the rest of our lives.

I'm sitting in Zanny's Wings waiting for Monica, Chandra and Chastity to get here. Every Sunday that we sing, we usually try to get together after church to catch up on what's going on with each of us. The only thing I've really got to share about is my mother. Every time I think about it, I got to shake my head.

I peek out the window again and I see everyone coming in the door. I get up from the seat and get in line so we can all order. We all say our hellos, order our food and take our seat next to one of the windows.

"My mother is tripping about wanting a man. You would think after dealing with Mr. Leroy that she wouldn't want nothing to do with any man for a long time." I bite into my tongue-torch wings.

"Yes, as scary as Mr. Leroy was I would stay clear of any man that said hello to me. She better check his history before she look at somebody twice. I'm just saying." Chandra says.

"Well, hopefully after she comes to church a couple of times, maybe she'll think differently." Monica adds.

"I hope so, but right after we got home from church she was talking about being alone. It's as if Michael and I aren't important."

"Maybe she just wants to be loved...I guess." Chastity laughs loudly.

"You stupid, girl!"

"I'm just keeping it real, Myra. I guess me and your mother are the opposite. She wants somebody and I don't want to be bothered; especially by Jonathan Berry."

"Is he still chasing after you?" Monica asks after taking a sip of her soda.

"Yes, but now he got the nerve to be flirting with Shayna Jefferson right in front of me. One minute he's texting me asking when we're going to do it again and when I say no, he starts sending her messages." Chastity takes a bite of her chicken fingers.

"Boys can be so trifling sometimes. It must be something that runs in their genes. I think Brian got a dose of trifling genes too." Chandra mentions.

"Not, Brian Miller, one of the best quarterbacks at Midland Central. I know he's not acting a fool too. Say it ain't so." Monica jokes.

"Girl, I wish I was joking because I really like Brian. Things were going real good with us, but before I came here to meet you guys he started talking real crazy."

"What was he saying?" I ask.

"He said we need to do more than what we're doing and I need to spend more time with him and we kiss like we're in the third grade."

"Oh boy, sounds like Mr. Quarterback wants to see your panties." I say and then I take another bite of one of my wings. Everyone else agrees with me by the nodding of their heads.

"Well, that ain't going down. I just don't want to get all caught up in that. He's getting this stuff from Tyrik Smalls." Chandra says as her left eyebrow raises.

"Tyrik Smalls? The boy that doesn't even come to school hardly? That is not good." I respond.

"I know. I'm trying to figure out why all of a sudden he's all up in Tyrik's face and listening to his advice. This is so not like Brian. I don't get it."

"And you probably will never get it because boys are straight crazy on all levels." Chastity says as she pops a fry in her mouth.

"Stop it, Chastity. They're not all crazy." I add.

"She might be right on that, Myra. I know Patrick has been acting kind of crazy too." Monica says.

"Are you sure it's Patrick that's acting crazy or have you slipped into crazy mode yourself?" Chandra asks.

"What do you mean by that Chandra?" I ask while looking back and forth between Chandra and Monica.

"You want me to tell them Monica or do you?" Chandra asks.

Monica lets out a long sigh and then starts explaining. "Well, this girl name Trena liked Patrick before me and so somebody approached me in the bathroom about it. I finally met up with her and she mentioned that she was going to try and get with Patrick and then I confronted him about it."

"And don't forget the part that you were about to fight the girl." Chandra adds.

"What? Not our lead singer in church?" I lean back in my chair because I can't believe Monica would be pushed to fight; especially over a boy.

"She came in my face first talking all that smack."

"What did Patrick have to say once you confronted him?" Chastity asks.

"He told me to calm down, but he did say that at one time he was trying to get with her, but she didn't give him a chance. She's brown skinned and small framed. She's a cheerleader."

"Oh, so she's trying to get back with him now?" I question.

"Yeah, it seems that way because of the things she said. I told him if he wanted that kind of girl he can go ahead and get her. It's fine with me." Monica throws down the rest of the fries that were in her hand.

"Girl, you need to stop! Patrick is probably not even thinking about this Trena chick." Chandra responds.

"Exactly. And what about all that stuff you told us that he's you're soul mate and one day you two are going to get married and all that." I rattle off.

"Yeah, well, if he don't do right by me, there won't be no wedding."

We all continue to talk about some more things going on at school and about our plans for singing. We all had a few things we were dealing with, but talking about it usually helps us through.

Chapter 12 – Monica

I'm in my third period class, which is Algebra. Chandra's in the same class with me. We sit across from one another. I'm trying to pay attention in class, but I can't get over thinking about this whole Trena and Patrick thing. I just can't shake it.

I haven't really talked to Patrick in a few days. He's been trying to call me over the weekend, but I've ignored his calls. He sent me a few text messages to tell me that he doesn't want to be with anybody else, but me. He keeps texting me to let me know that I don't have anything to worry about concerning Trena, but something tells me Trena doesn't feel that way.

I haven't seen her in the hallways in a while. I don't know if she's avoiding me or plotting to sneak up on me one day. I'm not really afraid of her because I know I could take her in a fight, but I know that isn't the right thing to do. I think what's really getting me is that she is prettier and thinner than me. As this thought enters my mind, another one comes right after it; *your black is beautiful and you are a beautiful black young lady. Your true beauty begins within and spreads out.* That is something that First Lady Rice would always tell me to repeat when I started thinking less of myself because of my skin color and my weight.

I have to shake these negative thoughts because I've been doing really well until Trena made those comments about my color and size.

As I continue to daydream and halfway listen to the teacher share about our next lesson, I feel Chandra tapping my foot with her foot. I look at her to see what's up. She points her finger to the doorway of the classroom. The door is open and standing in the hallway is Patrick. I look at him and smile. He smiles back and waves and then he moves his hands to tell me to come out to him.

I look at him, and then I look at Ms. Spivey and then back at Patrick. I know I'm not even listening to her lecture so I might as well hear what Patrick has to say. I raise my hand to ask to use the restroom.

Ms. Spivey excuses me and as I walk pass Chandra she whispers, "Be nice to him because he never said he wanted her now."

I nod my head and walk out the classroom. Patrick grabs me and hugs me and then takes my hand and I walk down the hall with him.

We're silent as we walk to the end of the hallway. We turn the corner and walk down another side of the hallway then Patrick grabs me and hugs me again. I let him and then he places his hand gently on the side of my face and leans in closer to kiss me on my lips. At first it's just a few pecks on my lips. I know I'm still a little upset with him, but I miss him too. So I let him keep kissing my lips and then he puts his tongue in my mouth. I let him kiss me, but then that little tingling feeling I get starts surfacing so I pull away from him.

"What do you want Patrick?" I manage to ask after breathing in and out.

"What do you mean, what do I want? I want you Lady Monica and you know that. Why haven't you answered my calls or responded to my text messages?"

I love it when Patrick calls me Lady Monica. It just does something to me because it still shows that he has the utmost respect for me. I know I like kissing him, but he already knows I'm the abstinence queen and I'm not about to bow down; not even to keep him away from Trena Lewis. She probably would jump at the chance to get Patrick in the bed. Those skinny, cheerleader type girls really get on my nerves.

"I just needed some time to think, Patrick. I mean you don't have to be with me if you don't want to. If Trena Lewis is what you really want, let me know now so I can get my feelings straight."

"I don't know why you keep thinking I want that girl, Monica!"

"Well, you wanted her before so I don't want to stop you now!"

"Monica, I don't get you. I'm telling you I don't want her. You're my girl and that's how I want it to be and you trying to push me off on her."

"I just don't want you to be with me just because you feel sorry for me or feel as though you're going to hurt my feelings. It's better for you to go ahead now before you break my heart later."

Patrick grabs me by my waist and pulls me closer to him. He kisses me again and I let him.

We stop and he says, "You better stop talking like that, girl. I mean what I say. I want to be with you and that's it."

"Well, what are you going to do when she keeps on trying to get with you because the last thing she said was that it wasn't over?"

"I'm not about to let that girl come between us and you better not either. And you better not fight her at school."

"She better leave me alone or this big girl gonna give her something to remember." I hold up my fist like I'm about to punch somebody in the head.

"Not my sweet Lady Monica. I know the gospel psalmist ain't about to step to nobody." Patrick laughs.

"It's not funny, Patrick." I smile back at him. I know I'm starting to sound like I'm crazy, but I'm not about to let Trena Lewis think she can take my boyfriend and beat me up too. Nope. It's not going to happen."

"You don't have nothing to worry about. Do you hear me?"

"I hear you."

As soon as I say that, Patrick's phone begins beeping to let him know he has a text message.

"You better turn that phone on vibrate before you get back to class. Your teacher is going to take your phone."

"Whatever, that ain't going to happen either." Patrick says as he pulls his phone out of his pocket. He looks at the phone and then his face changes. He looks as though he just bumped into a ghost or something.

"What's wrong? What is it?" I ask.

60

Patrick puts his phone back in his pocket real fast. He takes a deep breath. "Let me walk you back to class."

I don't move. Based on his look and his deep breath, I got to know what's on his phone. I know I'm bold, but he's my boyfriend so I'm going to ask him.

"What's on your phone?"

He responds with a short answer. "Nothing."

"Patrick you are lying. Tell me."

"You're going to get mad and I don't want to hear your mouth because I didn't tell her to do that."

"Her? Her who? Tell her to do what? Let me see your phone."

Before Patrick could respond, I grab for his phone out of his pocket and click on the message just sent. I know I looked the same way he did…..like I saw a ghost.

Only thing is this ghost had bare skin showing, breast showing and some really short, short, short, short shorts on. It was Trena Lewis and she sent a picture to Patrick telling him that he doesn't know what he's missing and that what she had was better than fat chocolate.

I drop Patrick's phone and I walk away from him. He's calling me to come back, but I'm ignoring him because by now the tears are coming down my face and I'm so mad I think I may have the ability to spit fire.

Chapter 13 – Chastity

"Chas I'm asking you one more time. You need to get back with me. You know you miss me and you know you want to do that again. So you down?"

I can't believe this same text message is coming on my phone. Doesn't Jonathan get it? I'm not doing anything with him. I'm good and I want to stay that way. I can't be bothered.

Yup, here we go again. We're sitting in our third period English class and Jonathan is sending me these crazy text messages again. Doesn't he know that no means no.

I see Shayna Jefferson look at me and then look at Jonathan to see if we're texting each other. Rumor has it that he had sex with her. He must think I'm a fool if he thinks he's going to have sex with me after he has had nasty ole Shayna Jefferson. That is definitely not going down; especially without being tested first.

Jonathan starts smiling at me and I shake my head, but apparently Shayna does not like what she sees because she gets up and stands in front of Jonathan's desk. Her weave is really tore down today. I don't know what she did with it, but hair is going in every direction and one place looks like it's all knotted up. It's just straight nasty. Her leggings are so tight I can actually see the print of the thong she's wearing. Really? A thong though? In school on a regular Wednesday? I got one word to describe all that…..nasty. Her shirt is right above her belly button so that doesn't help either. Did her mother let her leave the house like that? The sight of her makes me shake my head.

Somebody needs to definitely school her about the dress code policy at Midland Central High. She needs some assistance in a lot of ways. She needs to meet First Lady Rice. I know First Lady Rice would set her straight and she would do it in love. Right now, I'm not feeling all that anxious about showing her some love; especially since she's having sex with Jonathan.

I hear the two of them exchanging words with one another. Shayna is trying to whisper, but it is very clear that she doesn't know how to do that.

"Why you looking at her?" She says to Jonathan while rolling her neck.

"Yo, chill Shayna. You need to sit down." Jonathan replies.

"Don't think you going do me and her too."

"Ain't nobody doing anything. Just chill." Jonathan says while trying to push Shayna away from him to get her to sit down.

Shayna got the hint and starts walking back to her seat, but she didn't stop popping off at the mouth.

"I know you ain't doing nothing because I got this and you know you want this." Shayna said as she pointed to her most sacred female area below her waist.

My eyes widen and so does Jonathan's. He had no idea who he was dealing with. Shayna was straight ghetto and she didn't mind letting you know it. I know Jonathan is wishing he had never messed up with me because I'm a good girl. At least I got some class about me. Shayna is just trifling. I smile and then I let out a short laugh.

A smile is locked on my face until I feel my phone vibrating in my jeans pocket. I jump slightly because it scared me. I reach in my pocket to read the text. I know it's from Jonathan.

"So you think that's real funny don't you. You got me on that one. Shayna is crazy! Straight up....I miss you Chas."

I laugh a little, but then I stop when I finish reading the rest of the text. It's good to read that Jonathan misses me. I guess he's finally recognizing what he had. The truth is I miss him too, but I'm not so sure I can take him back at this point. I got standards to live by and sex ain't included in them. I send him a text back.

"I miss you too Jonathan. I miss hanging out with you, but I think its best we just remain friends for now."

I glance over at Jonathan as he's reading my text. He smiles and then his smile turns into a frown. He lets out a deep sigh and then Shayna says something out loud.

"You better leave my man alone."

I guess she's talking to me, but I'm thinking, what man is she talking about because Jonathan sure ain't no man. Especially since he couldn't man up when I thought I was pregnant. I'm not about to be moved by Ms. Ghettofabulista.

Jonathan realizes she's talking to me too so he snaps his figures to get her attention. She rolls her eyes at me and then turns her head to acknowledge his snap. He points his index finger at her and says, "Chill right now."

Shayna sucks her teeth and rolls her neck, but she keeps quiet and starts working. The way Jonathan snapped his figures and told her to chill you would have thought she was his puppy

65

dog. When are these boys going to learn how to talk right to girls? I guess I have to look at it that Jonathan was really looking out for me. He may have messed up with me, but he wasn't about to let anyone else mess with his *Chas*. I text him back despite Shayna's remark.

"Your girl is CRAZY! She need Jesus....bad. Thanks for looking out."

"LOL. I'll always look out for you Chas. I need you to know that if you're not going to give me another chance, I'm about to do something I really don't want to."

"Jonathan, why do you keep saying that? You sound like you're going try to commit suicide or something? Don't be fool!"

"Chill. Just tell me what your answer is. You gonna give us another chance?"

"Jonathan, let's just keep it the way it is for now."

"Alright, if that's how you want to be. I guess I got to do what I got to do."

Before I could send another text, the bell rings. Everybody gets up from their seats. Shayna grabs Jonathan's arm so quick I can't even get a chance to say anything else to him. I really want to know more about what he was talking about. I got a funny feeling about it all. I didn't before, but since he brought it up again I'm starting to wonder what this is all about. I hope he doesn't do anything stupid to hurt himself. That would really make me feel bad.

Chapter 14 – Myra

"There go my girl." Xavier walks up from behind me and wraps his arms around my waist while I'm looking for something in my locker. He kisses me on my cheek.

"Hey, how are you doing, Xavier?"

"I'm good now that I see you." He smiles at me and of course I smile back. I know I'm blushing. It becomes so obvious with light brown skin.

"Where are you about to go?"

"I'm about to go back to my class. I stepped out because I had to go to the restroom, but I don't have to go back right away if you want to chill for a while."

I smile again because I know what Xavier means when he wants to chill for a while. He wants to kiss and not just the basic peck on the lips or kiss on the cheek kissing; he wants our lips, mouths and tongues to make a connection.

Xavier is good to me and nothing like my ex-boyfriend, Larry. They are total opposites. I don't mind kissing him, but I try not to let him kiss me like that too much because my body reacts to it; especially in my private area. I know I'm not a virgin anymore since I let Larry convince me to have sex with him; actually he practically forced me, but I'm not so sure I want to go down that path again. It was not a good experience for me and I think it was just too much to handle. The whole relationship with Larry was too much to handle and I'm so glad I'm out of that crazy relationship.

If I was going to have sex, Xavier would definitely be my choice if I was interested, but for some reason my thoughts often go back to what First Lady Rice tells us about waiting until we get married.

I don't know if Xavier is all up to waiting until marriage to have sex with me because I don't know if we will even be together that long. I know he hasn't pressured me, but I got this feeling he wishes things would be a little different between us.

"You know I got to get back to class."

"Yeah, but you out here now getting your books so just let your teacher know you had to make a stop to the bathroom too."

I smile. I know where this is going and I know what we're going to end up doing.

"Boy, you ain't slick."

"I'm not trying to be. You know what time it is Myra."

I take a deep breath, shut my locker door and start walking. Xavier puts his arm around my shoulder and we continue to talk as we walk back around to the back part of the school where hardly any administrators monitor.

When we get to our usual spot, Xavier grabs my books from out of my hands and places them on the floor next to us. I breathe in and out because I know we're going to kiss. I like kissing Xavier. He moves in closer to me and puts his hands around my waist. I lift my arms up, place them around his neck and then the kissing begins.

At first it feels very gentle and then our kissing gets intense. It's becoming so intense that I feel Xavier's hand squeezing my butt and then he gradually takes his hand and starts feeling on my breast.

I pull away from him. "Xavier, we better stop."

"What's wrong Myra? You know you my girl."

"I know, but I don't feel right doing this here." I wanted to say I didn't feel right doing this anywhere, but I didn't want to offend him.

"Cool. I understand. I don't want to disrespect you, but I'm just can't help myself around you." Xavier grabs me and gives me a hug.

"Thank you for showing me some respect." I know Xavier was a good person and he's always been respectful, but I think his hormones are trying to shift his character a bit.

"Yeah, I told you I know how to treat a lady."

"Okay, but for a minute there you reminded me of Larry and how he used to force himself on me."

"I'm not backing up Larry, but he probably couldn't help it because you're so pretty. I don't know what it is, but lately I just can't keep my hands off you." Xavier smiles at me.

"Whatever! I just know I don't want to be forced to do anything I don't want to. I let Larry trip me up with that because I didn't want to offend him or get him upset. All I know is; I *got to do better*."

"Oh it will be better with me." Xavier sneaks another kiss on my lips.

I cross my arms around my chest and lean my head to the side as if I'm about to tell Xavier off. I got a few words I can share, but what stops me is when I see these two guys walking down the hall towards us in my peripheral vision.

As they walk closer I notice it's Tyrik Smalls and Brian Miller. I don't know why they are talking together, but something just doesn't seem right. Brian is not the kind of guy that would hang around Tyrik. Tyrik is into drugs, cutting school and just up to no good. Wait until I tell Chandra this. I remember her telling us how she is suspicious of these two talking and I'm starting to feel the same way.

"Hello, are you there?" Xavier is waving his hand back and forth in front of my face. I totally forgot he was standing there. That's what being nosey will do for you; tune you out of what's going on in your own life. I laugh at him.

"I'm sorry. Shhhhh." I cover Xavier's mouth because I know he's going to say what's up, but I wanted to watch Brian and Tyrik a little more. I point over to their direction and whisper to tell him to continue to be quiet.

I was trying my best to hear their conversation, but all I could make out was Tyrik telling Brian that he better get that and if she kept playing hard like she wasn't down then he had something he could use.

What were they talking about? Get what? And what did he have for him to use and who was Tyrik suggesting that Brian should use it on? Something ain't right.

Chapter 15 – Monica

By the time I'm walking back to get to my classroom, the tears are slowing down from falling down my cheeks. I can't believe this. I can't escape the fact that I know Patrick and I belong together, but I will not accept him being with me and getting with Trena too. Sharing my boyfriend is not one of the standards that I live by. I know; I know we're only in high school, but sometimes beautiful marriages are birthed from high school sweethearts. I'm just saying. I can't let that skinny little cheerleader, Trena Lewis block my blessing. This is just too much for me. My heart is racing and I know I better chill before my heart pops out of my chest.

I walk back in class with my head slightly down so nobody will notice my tears. As I'm walking pass Chandra, she grabs my hand to stop me in my tracks. I look up at her and stare at her as if I've been abused for many years.

She whispers, "What happened?"

"It's a mess. It's worse than I thought. This Trena chick is trying to be a porn star too."

Chandra gasps. I keep walking back to my seat because I don't want the teacher to call us out and embarrass us for talking in class.

I sit down. The teacher is talking, but I declare I have no clue as to what she is saying. To keep it real, I don't care what she's saying at this point. The only thing on my mind is Patrick and this crazy porn queen Trena Lewis. This mess has got to stop. I'm either going to have to set her straight or I may have to give in to some drastic measures to keep Patrick.

The things I'm thinking about right now aren't right, but I just don't want to lose Patrick. I know I shouldn't beg someone to stay with me, but I never really had a boyfriend before because nobody really wanted to be with me. It was either my size or my color that seemed to cause boys to turn the other way. Patrick is different; or at least I thought he was.

Chandra throws a piece of paper at me to take me out my trance. I look her way.

"What's up?" She tries to whisper, but she is having difficulty because the teacher responds.

"What's up with what, Ms. Mitchell?" The teacher stops in the middle of her lesson.

Chandra doesn't respond at first because she definitely doesn't want to get written up. So she plays it off.

"Oh, I was just thinking about the problem you were talking about and was wondering what was up with the….." Chandra's sentence trails because I guess she couldn't come up with a good lie.

I chuckle a little.

"Ms. Mitchell, please make sure you pay attention and not chit chat with your friends during class. Thank you."

"Yes ma'am." Chandra says and then looks over at me and smiles.

I know she wants to know what's going on with me, but it's too much to share with my inside voice. She'll just have to wait until the bell rings to hear this hot gossip.

Chapter 16 – Monica

As soon as we walk out of class, Chandra hits me up with the questions about what happened with Patrick. I share with her what happened and she is almost speechless.

"I can't believe she is that bold. Is it that serious?" Chandra asks.

"Obviously to her it is."

"What are you going to do? I mean I know you're not going to do anything crazy."

I look at Chandra with a blank stare as if to say crazy actions deserve crazy responses. I know I'm not going to be silent about this. I can't. I got to say something to Trena Lewis because I can't just let her think she can send naked pictures to my boyfriend on a regular.

Something really has to be done about these girls who stoop to this level. I mean sharing a picture of you naked is a bit desperate.

"Girl, I don't know what I'm going to do yet, but I got to do something. I can't let her think she can do that and get away with it."

"I hear you Monica, but don't do anything to get you kicked out of school."

I breathe in and out before I respond. "I hear you Chandra, but this girl is a trip."

"Well, maybe you should talk with Patrick first before you go off on Trena Lewis. I mean girls always go off on the girl and don't address the boy."

"True, but Patrick didn't ask her to send him that picture….at least I don't think so."

"Maybe he didn't…..or maybe he did." Chandra says.

"Well, if he knows like I know he better not have asked her to send that naked picture of her." I can feel my heart beat beginning to speed up just at the thought of Patrick being the one asking for the naked picture of Trena Lewis. All I know is he better not have asked or it's going to be on.

"Okay, try to remain calm. Think about it; Patrick doesn't seem like the type to go behind your back and ask Trena that."

"Yeah, but I didn't even know Trena was even Patrick's type anyway. So ain't no telling what else he got up his sleeve."

As Chandra and I continue to talk, I see about four girls coming our way. They're just walking, talking and laughing amongst themselves, but the closer I look I recognize one of the girls very clearly. It's Trena Lewis and some of her skinny cheerleading friends. As far as I'm concerned they're probably all porn stars on the sneak tip.

I hear Chandra's voice, but I have no idea what's coming out of her mouth because all I'm focusing on is Trena and her friends that are about to pass us.

"Monica, Monica….do you hear me talking to you?" Chandra is yelling at this point.

I shake out of my trance. "Yeah, I hear you, but my eyes are on them." I directed my eyes towards Trena and her friends. I didn't want to point because I didn't want her to think I was the least bit intimidated by her. Even though her curves were more defined and mine were……well I didn't have real curves, but I had enough meat on my bones to keep warm without a coat. I'm just saying my weight helps during the cold weather.

Chandra slowly turns her head to see what I'm talking about.

"That's her?"

"Yup, that's the porn queen."

Before we can continue with our conversation, I hear these words, "He don't want none of that fat meat!"

It was Trena Lewis talking smack in front of her friends. They all start laughing. My right eyebrow raises and sweat beads are forming on top of my lip. I'm trying to remain calm.

"I know she's not talking to you, is she?" Chandra asks.

"She better not be, but I got a feeling she is." I manage to say as my hands are forming into fists.

"I know you heard me black girl! Fat and black. That's what you are. I don't know why Patrick wants you."

That's it. My feet move faster than they ever have. You would have thought I ran track every day. I'm heading towards Trena's direction with Chandra walking real fast behind him.

I stand right in front of Trena's face and for some reason I freeze in one spot. Not because I'm scared, but because I hear a little voice in my head say, *you know better than that. You can't let her get to you. You got to do better. Don't stoop to her level.*

"What you going do?" Trena boasts.

People start to crowd around us. I don't know why they are, but I guess because how we're looking at each other and the way we're standing so close to each other. Our body language was clearly telling everyone passing by to stop and see what was going on.

As the crowd grew, the voice disappears, I pull my fist back, and before I could release it. Someone grabs it in midair.

"Okay, Monica come with me." It's Mrs. Porter. She kindly put her arm on my shoulder and turns me around. She then tells everyone else to get back to class. She walks me to her classroom and Chandra follows us.

As we were walking away I could hear, Mr. Carter, one of the school administrators telling everyone to clear the hallways and to go to their classrooms.

When we got to Mrs. Porter's classroom, she began drilling me with questions.

"So what in the world is going on Monica?"

"She was talking smack and I didn't want to hear her mouth anymore. Plus….." The rest of my sentence trails as Mrs. Porter interrupts.

"Since when have you become a fighter? Do you know you can get put out of school? Now, I'm going to have to write you up."

"But Mrs. Porter, you don't understand. She has been calling me names and then sending my boyfriend pictures and…."

"Monica, I know this isn't all about a boy?" Mrs. Porter asks while she's pulling out a referral to write on.

"Mrs. Porter, you're not listening." The tears are forming in my eyes. Chandra places her hand on my shoulder.

"Mrs. Porter, Monica is being harassed by this girl because of her boyfriend Patrick. She's calling her names and sending crazy pictures to Patrick. I heard her call Monica, 'black and fat' while she was with her friends."

"Thank you for sharing that Chandra, but Monica and I have already had this talk about not worrying and reacting to other people calling her names. She has to know that she's beautiful no matter what others think."

"It's not that Mrs. Porter. I'm good with how I look. This girl just keeps coming at me and my boyfriend and I just lost it."

"Well, losing it is going to cost you two days out of school." As Mrs. Porter continues to write on the referral, Mr. Carter walks in.

"Mrs. Porter, I hope you're writing up this young lady. We can't have this kind of disturbance in our school."

"Yes, sir. I'm filling out the paperwork now."

"Good. She's going to have to be out for two days suspension. The other girl will get in-school suspension the rest of the day and tomorrow."

Mr. Carter then turns to me. "I don't know what got you so upset young lady, but that kind of behavior is not accepted at Midland Central. Hopefully these two days will calm you down and help you realize that this wasn't worth it at all."

Mrs. Porter looked at me and then looked at Mr. Carter. "Thank Mr. Carter. I'll make sure I send the paperwork to your office and call her parent so that she can pick her up."

"Sounds good Mrs. Porter. Thank you for making sure this didn't go any further than it did." Mr. Carter turns and walks out of the classroom.

As soon as Mr. Carter closes the door to Mrs. Porter's room, Chandra and I both look at each other. And then we blurt out, "Mrs. Porter!"

"I'm sorry girls there is nothing I can do. Mr. Carter was near by the incident and I knew I was going to have to write you up especially since everyone was crowding around. I hate to do this Monica, but you can't let these girls get you so upset over stuff you have no control over."

"Okay, Mrs. Porter. I understand."

"Good. Now sign this referral and dial your mother's phone number so I can tell her to come pick you up."

Dialing my mother to tell her that I was going to be put out of school was not something I was in a hurry to do. I know she was going to be upset about this especially when the whole thing is about someone calling me names and because we were arguing over a boy. Well, not just any boy, it was Patrick; my soul mate. I hope my mother understands.

78

Chapter 17 – Monica

My mother picks me up from the school after Mrs. Porter calls her and informs her that I've been suspended from school for two days. We're driving in the car on the way home. My mother is a bit upset that she had to leave work to get me.

"Monica, you got to be kidding me. You mean to tell me you got put out of school for almost fighting a girl over Patrick?"

"Well, partly yes and partly no."

"What does that mean, Monica?"

"Well, she started calling me names and….." I start to respond until my mother interrupts me.

"Don't you dare tell me this has something to do with being called names because of the color of your skin? We've already been through this before, Monica."

"I know. I know, but it's more to it than that."

"Oh yeah, it's about Patrick." My mother says with so much sarcasm in her voice that it was almost offensive.

She had no idea how upset I was. Not just about Trena Lewis calling me black and fat, but because of those pictures that she sent of herself to Patrick. Now, I'm going to be out of school for two days and I didn't even get a chance to really talk with Patrick about those pictures. Not only that, I'm going to be out for two days and she'll probably be all up in his face.

"Mom, you don't understand. She is trying to come between me and Patrick."

"And?" My mother looks at me, raises her eyebrow and then turns her direction back to driving and focusing on the road.

"Mom! You know Patrick is my boyfriend and he's really nice to me."

"Monica, if Patrick is your boyfriend and he's really that nice and respectful to you, then you have nothing to worry about. However, you got to realize that boys will be boys. You two are still young. Not all boys are ready to totally commit to one girl. Let's face it, both of you are too young to commit like that."

"Mom, in case you didn't know Patrick is my soul mate and I don't want to be with anyone else, but him and he feels the same way about me and I'm not about to let this skinny chick, Trena Lewis come between that."

My mother starts laughing and continues to do so for a long time. She laughed so much that her whole body shook. After gasping for air, she finally says, "Monica Ellington you got a lot to learn about relationships, love and soul mates so don't get so caught up in one boy when you got a whole life ahead of you. Like I said before, if Patrick is as serious as you say he is, you have no worries. I just don't want you to get so caught up and get your feelings hurt more than what they are now. And, I definitely don't want you to get put out of school over no boy. Do you understand that?"

"Yes ma'am." That's all I'm saying to my mother from now on about Patrick because obviously she doesn't understand my true feelings for Patrick. After listening to my mother, I just hope Patrick still feels the same way; especially after seeing those naked pictures of Trena Lewis on his phone. I wonder did he erase those pictures. He better have or else I'm going to stomp him.

Chapter 18 – Brian

I'm on my way to lunch to meet up with Chandra, but as I'm walking, I see Tyrik Smalls coming down the hallway towards me. He's waving his hand at me to tell me to catch up with him.

"Hey, what's up?" Tyrik says as he daps me up.

"I'm good. What's up with you?"

"Nothing. I was thinking about the last time we talked about you and your girl. Man, you ain't hit that yet?"

"Naw, man. It ain't like that. We just started really going together since football season."

"She you're girl, right?"

"Yeah, she's my girl. We've been kicking it for a couple of months."

"I don't get it then. You should have got that by now."

"Man, we taking it slow, but….." I stop myself because I didn't know what else to say. It's hard to tell another brother that you not having sex with your girl; especially someone like Tyrik Smalls. Plus everyone knows I'm one of the quarterbacks at Midland Central and I can get any girl I want and have sex with a few of them if I wanted to just because I play on the team. There are a lot of cheerleaders ready to spread their legs for a boy on the football team if we're down for it.

"Slow? Since when does the main Quarterback at Midland Central take it slow? You supposed to handle the ball quickly. What's up you scared?"

"Man, no. Chandra is a church girl so I got to move slowly with her." I squirm a little on the inside because deep down I'm a church boy too. Born and raised in the church, but my male hormones got a whole different agenda than abstinence. Tyrik is right. It's time out for this slow stuff.

"Oh, that's what it is. I got something that will work to fix that. She won't even know what hit her."

"What you talking about Tyrik?"

"Man, it's something you can slip in her drink that will make her pass out and when she does, you can take it. She won't even know what happened."

"You talkin' about using drugs?!"

"Man, don't look it like that. She not going get hooked on it or nothing like that. It will just help her give you what you want. You want it don't you?"

I didn't respond because I wasn't so sure what Tyrik was up to or if I wanted to do that to Chandra. She's my girl and all and I have the utmost respect for her and I really want to take it slow, but on the flip side I can't let Tyrik think I'm not down with getting with Chandra in a sexual way. Quarterbacks just don't back down; it's not in their nature.

"So what's up? You want it or don't you? You scared." Tyrik teases.

"No, I'm not scared. Tell me about this and how it works."

Tyrik began to describe to me about this pill I could drop in Chandra's drink and it would dissolve on its own. All I had to do was get her to drink it and in a matter of minutes she would black out. It would give me enough time to get her clothes off and have sex with her. No doubt, I do want to get with Chandra like that, but I know she really isn't down for that so I haven't pressured her about it, but maybe it's time I do.

"So, that's all I got to do?"

"Yeah that's it. Invite her over your house or somebody's house and do your thang. I can even have a private party and invite you two over and you can use a room in my house because my mom works at night."

"Alright. Let me think about it and see when I want to do that." I reply.

"Alright, man don't wait too long. It's past time for you to get that."

I dap Tyrik, he walks down the hall, and I walk down the other hallway. I see Chandra coming down the hallway looking for me. I walk towards her so we can eat lunch together. I wonder what's going to happen to us after I do this.

Chapter 19 – Myra

While I'm working on my homework, my cell phone goes off. I see that it's Chandra calling me. She was supposed to give me the scoop on what happened with Monica today in school with that Trena girl.

"Hey, Chandra. What's up?"

"Nothing. I just wanted to call you to give you the details on what happened with Monica. She is so upset. I just got off the phone with her and she wanted me to give you the details."

"Okay, so what happened?" I put my pencil down because I knew I wasn't about to continue with writing my English essay that was due tomorrow. It would have to wait until I got this piece of gossip on my girl, Monica.

"When we got out of class, Trena and her crew were coming up the hallway. Trena started calling Monica names and she lost it."

"Girl, I can't believe Monica lost her cool like that."

"Yeah, I know. She may get upset sometimes, but she's definitely not the fighting type, but I guess she got tired of it."

"Yeah, but Chandra why did she get so mad about her calling her names? You know we already told her to not let that bother her especially from Trena Lewis. She already knows she wants to try to get Patrick back."

"Yeah, but I guess after she found out about the pictures that Trena sent Patrick, it pushed her over the edge."

"Pictures? What pictures?" I ask as I stand up from my bed and start pacing my floor. I didn't hear about any pictures so I didn't know what Chandra was talking about.

"Myra, you are not going to believe this, but that crazy Trena Lewis sent naked pictures of herself to Patrick on his cell phone. When Monica was talking to him in the hallway, the text came through his phone. Monica grabbed the phone and it was pictures of Trena."

"Oh Lord! What did Patrick say?" I ask.

"I don't know. I guess he was trying to explain to her that he didn't ask her to do that, but Monica was not hearing it. So I don't know if he even had a chance to say any more about it."

"Wow! I hope he says something to her while she's out. I wonder if her mother is going to let Patrick come and visit her now."

"I don't know. You know Mrs. Ellington don't play. Monica already said her mother gave her the speech about worrying about the name calling and about her saying Patrick is her soul mate." Chandra lets out a laugh.

"Monica is a trip! She's even telling that to her mother?"

"Yup!" Chandra laughed more and so did I.

Monica Ellington was adamant about Patrick being her soul mate and she wasn't about to let anyone tell her differently; not even her own mother. I just hope that Trena Lewis understands that too.

"So did they actually fight? And how long is she going to be out of school?"

"No, before Monica could punch Trena in the face, Mrs. Porter grabbed Monica's arm and blocked her swing. She got written up for two days out of school, but Trena got in school suspension."

"That ain't fair. Trena should have got put out too since she started it with her big mouth." I respond as I sit back down on my bed.

"Yeah, I know, but because she was about to swing on her, she got the days out."

"Well, I guess we'll see what happens after this because this has got to stop. Patrick is going have to do something and Monica is going to have to chill."

"Yeah he is and she does. You know we got this concert coming up at the school because they're doing a Gospel Extravaganza and we got our annual church concert that we have to perform in three weeks so she better get right."

"You are right Chandra, she definitely *got to do better*. She's the lead vocalist and we can't have our lead vocalist throwing blows instead of hitting those melodious notes with her voice. It just doesn't match." I laugh, but I was for real.

"For real."

"Well, let me get off this phone because I got to finish this essay for English and plus my mother is going out on a date tonight with some guy she met and she wants me to cook something for me and my brother."

"Oh really. So she's dating again?"

"Yeah, I guess so. I've been trying to get her to come back to church again, but she acts like she's not interested. She came a few times, but all of a sudden she stopped once she started dating this guy."

"Well, Myra, I hope he's not crazy. I don't mean no harm, but after what happened with Mr. Leroy I wouldn't want my mother dating again for a long time."

"Exactly. I was trying to convince her to fall in love with Jesus, but she wants some real arms around her waist. So there you have it." I chuckle.

"Girl, you crazy!"

"Let me go. I'll chat with you later."

"Okay, Myra. See you tomorrow."

"Okay. Bye."

Chapter 20 – Chastity

I'm not having sex with nobody. Not going down that road anymore until I'm ready for all that follows, which means it's most likely going to take place when I get married. So my next boyfriend is just going to have to accept that because that's how it's going to be. It's time to really live up to the true meaning of my name.

The semester has changed and I'm sitting in one of my new classes, which happens to be health education. Today, we just so happen to be talking about sex education and the consequences of it. Some of the students are paying attention and some of the other students are laughing.

After the teacher finishes with her discussion she tells us to get in groups of four. We all get up from our seats and move to the other side of the class with a group of four.

A girl and two boys come to the area I'm sitting at. They pull their chairs near me. One of the boys is talking to the girl. I guess they know each other. The other boy pulls his chair next to me.

"Hey, my name is Jason. What's yours?"

"Hi, I'm Chastity."

"Good to meet you Chastity." He smiles at me. I notice that his teeth are very nice.

"I haven't seen you around. Are you new here?"

"Yeah, I just moved here from Maryland. My dad is in the military."

"Oh, okay. That's cool. Welcome to Midland Central."

"Thanks." He smiles again, but this time he winks his eye at me.

The teacher takes a minute to give some instructions on what we have to do in our group so my conversation with Jason ends abruptly and he is moving to another group, but I have a feeling Jason has more to say based on that wink and his nice smile.

"Okay class, let's begin finishing up with your book review project for today. Before you leave I want you to go to at least one other person in another group and begin to share what your group is working on."

I stare at the teacher for a few minutes because I wasn't sure who I was going to go to, but I was hoping that Jason would approach me. I turn my head to my left and Jason starts walking towards me.

"I thought I wasn't going to get a chance to talk with you before we left class."

"Oh yeah. What did you want to talk with me about?" I try not to blush, but Jason is grinning from ear-to-ear.

"I was just hoping that we could talk again since I really don't know anyone around here. Plus.....you're cute." Jason grins.

I laugh a little first before answering him. "You are funny, but thank you. Well, if you want me to show you around I can do that."

"That sounds real good. Do you want to eat lunch together? Then you can fill me in on what goes on here at Midland Central."

"I guess that would be okay."

"You guess? What's the matter, your boyfriend won't like it?"

"First of all, I don't have a boyfriend. I usually eat with my friends, but I guess just this once will be fine."

"That's good. So where should I meet you?"

"Well, we got one more class before we go to lunch so let's just meet in front of the cafeteria and then we can decide where we're going to sit. I hope you like school cafeteria food. Sometimes it's nasty!"

Jason laughs. "I'm sure they can't mess up a hamburger and French fries."

"Humph, you haven't been in Midland Central's cafeteria. You better hope that hamburger ain't burnt and those French fries are cooked all the way."

"Dang, it's that bad?"

"You'll see. You better get a slice a pizza that's about the only thing decent."

"Well, as long as I get to sit with you that's all that matters." Jason smiles.

All I can do is smile back at him. He has such a nice smile and he isn't hard to look at either.

The teacher interrupts us again and tells us it was time to get our things packed up so we can go to our next class. I guess I'm going to have to see what Jason is into when we eat lunch together.

Chapter 21 – Patrick

I'm sitting in the cafeteria by myself and missing my girl, Monica. Usually we eat lunch together, but because she's going to be out for two days I guess I have to sit alone these two days. I hate that Monica isn't going to be here. This whole thing with Trena has got to stop. Monica needs to get it through her thick skull that I don't want to be with Trena; I want to be with her. After all, I tried being with Trena and she acted like I wasn't good enough for her.

I got to admit Trena really looked good in those pictures she sent me. At first, I wasn't going to erase them because they looked so good, but I know that would only start more drama between me and Monica. Trena should have got me when she had a chance.

Trena would really have to come correct if she would ever get a chance with me. I mean she's fine and all that, but her attitude would definitely have to tone down. As I'm taking a bite of my pizza, I feel this hand on my back. I turn around.

"Hey, Patrick. I finally get a chance to talk with you alone."

It's Trena. She leans her breast on my shoulder and gives me a quick kiss on the cheek. I drop my pizza on my tray.

"Trena, what are you doing?"

"Something I should have done a long time ago when I first saw you."

"Well, it's too late for that now. Plus, aren't you supposed to be at in-school suspension?"

93

"Better late than never; I always say. I walked out of in-school suspension for a minute so I could find you. I told them I had to go to the bathroom." Trena sits down real close to me.

I move to my left slightly before responding to her. "That's cool Trena, but like I said it's a bit late for you and me."

"I know you can't be serious Patrick. You gonna pass all this up for that fat, black chocolate girl?"

"I'm going to need you to stop talking about my girl like that. Case you didn't realize I'm the same color as her and much bigger than her."

"Yeah, that's why you need some of this caramel to mix with that dark chocolate. Our babies will come out better."

"Babies? Girl, I ain't about to have no babies and if I do it won't be with you."

"Yeah you say that now, but I know I can change your mind." Trena leans in closer to me and kisses my lips.

"So what in the ham sandwich are you doing, Patrick? I know you not doing my girl like that!" Chandra says while her hands are on her hips.

I push back from Trena. I definitely didn't want to give the impression to Trena or Chandra that I was enjoying this. Trena is bold and doesn't care what anyone says. She's going to go after what she wants no matter what.

"There's nothing going on Chandra. Really....." My voice trails because Trena interrupts me.

"They ain't nothing going on now, but you know I'll see you later at my house after school. It'll be a lot going on then." Trena puts her hand on my chest and then walks away. She purposely bumps into Chandra.

"Oh you don't want none of this trick." Chandra responds.

Trena keeps walking out of the cafeteria, and leaves me and Chandra there.

"There is nothing going on Chandra. She just caught me off guard. That's it."

"Okay so first she's sending naked pictures of herself and now she's getting bold by kissing and touching on you while my girl, Monica ain't here. I don't like it Patrick and you better not be doing nothing with her."

"Chill. I'm not doing nothing. I don't want her."

"Well, it didn't look that way when I walked up on the two of you. Looked like to me you were enjoying her lips on yours."

"I didn't kiss her back. She just put her lips on mine."

"Monica is not going to believe that when I tell her."

"Wait, Chandra. Why do you have to tell Monica? You know she's going to be upset and want to fight me and Trena. Don't do that."

"I got to tell her, Patrick. She's my friend and if something like this happened with Brian, I would want someone to tell me."

"Yeah, but what you're going to tell her is not all the truth. I don't want Trena. Trena should have got me when she had the chance. You know I want to be with Monica and nobody else."

"Well, if you want Monica so bad then keep your lips off of Trena."

"I will. So you gonna tell her?"

"Yeah, I'm going to tell her."

Before I could say anything else, Chandra walks away and sits at the table with the rest of Monica's friends. This is not going to be good. Monica is going to flip the script.

Chapter 22 – Chastity

Chandra comes running over to me like she's upset about something.

"Chandra, what's wrong?"

"Girl, Patrick done lost his mind. He can't be doing our girl, Monica like that."

"What did he do?"

"I'll have to fill you in, but it definitely didn't look good. You sitting with us for lunch?" Chandra asks while putting food on her tray.

"No, I think I'm going to sit with this new boy I met in my class. His family is military and they just moved here. He doesn't really know anybody so he asks to have lunch with me."

"Oh yeah, what's his name?"

"His name is Jason. I don't know his last name."

"Oh okay. Is he cute?"

"Girl, yes!" I laugh as I pick up my juice to go with my pizza.

As soon as Chandra and I turn around after getting our food, I notice that Jason is standing right in front of me. He smiles and I smile back at him.

"So were you looking for me?" He asks.

"I was about to." We stare at each other for a few minutes before I feel Chandra nudging me with her elbow.

"Oh yeah, this is my friend, Chandra. Chandra this is Jason. He's in my class and his family is military so he's new to Midland Central."

"Nice to meet you Jason. And what is your last name? And where are you originally from?" Chandra asks like she's some type of private investigator.

He laughs a little and so do I. "Good to meet you too. My last name is Wright. My name is Jason Wright and I'm originally from Maryland."

"Oh okay. Welcome to Midland Central. Well, I guess I'll see you around. Make sure you're nice to my girl, Chastity."

"Most definitely. That's exactly what I plan to do." Jason smiles at me and winks at me again. I just blush. I don't know why, but I do.

Chandra walks away from us and I'm still standing in front of Jason, holding my tray and not knowing what exactly to say. He must have felt the long pause also so he starts up the conversation.

"How about I go find some of that pizza and you find us a place to sit together."

I look around the cafeteria to see if I can spot a table before walking away from him. I saw one of the small tables that is set for two people by the window.

I point in the direction of the table. "I'll meet you over there by the window."

"Perfect. Be there in a few."

I walk away slowly from Jason and push through the crowd to get to the table before someone else does. I place my tray on the table and take a quick glance around the cafeteria.

I see Jonathan. He doesn't see me at first, but then when I look up again; we lock eyes. He's walking with Shayna who has her arm wrapped around his.

I turn away when I see Jason standing in front of me. "Are you alright?" He asks.

"Yes, I'm cool. Have a seat."

Jason sits down across from me. I glance back over at Jonathan and Shayna and notice the look on Jonathan's face. He's frowning. Jason interrupts my trance again.

"So are you going to say anything to me or are you just going to stare at everyone in the cafeteria?"

I laugh slightly. "I'm sorry Jason. I don't mean to be rude and yes I'll say stuff to you. You have my undivided attention."

"Good. Excuse me for a minute." Jason bows his head slightly, closes his eyes and his lips start moving. It's in a low whisper, but I believe he's praying. Wow, that's cool.

After he finishes he says, "I always say my grace since I was a kid. My mom used to make me so now it's something I do all the time."

"That's cool. There is nothing wrong with that. Do you go to church?"

"When I was in Maryland we did, but we haven't been to church since we've been here. My parents said we were going to go visit some churches."

"Good. Maybe you can come visit my church, New Beginnings Christian Center. Our pastor can preeeeach! And our First Lady is awesome!"

"Sounds like you really like your church."

"Yeah, I do." I smile at Jason and he smiles back at me. It seemed like an hour went by as we continue to look at each other. Our trance ended abruptly when someone stood alongside our table.

"So this what you doing now Chas? You got you a new man now?"

"Jonathan you need to chill. We're just having lunch."

"Yeah, whatever."

"Is this your boyfriend?" Jason asks me without even looking up at Jonathan.

"Yeah I'm her boyfriend and you better step."

"You are not my boyfriend!" I yell.

"Dag man. Sounds like to me she doesn't want nothing to do with you. What you do?" Jason smiles slightly at me and then winks at me. He grabs his carton of milk to take a sip.

I smile back at him. Apparently Jonathan doesn't like me smiling at somebody else.

Jonathan pushes the milk carton out of Jason's hand. Jason immediately jumps up and pushes Jonathan.

"If you want to do something, step outside." Jason says while all up in Jonathan's face.

"Man, we can do this right here." Jonathan yells back.

I get in between them.

"Jonathan, stop playing before you both get kicked out of school." By then people are starting to look at the three of us. Some people were walking over to see what they could hear.

"You need to tell this dude to step. You're my girl!" Jonathan responds.

"I am not your girl! Stop saying that and just walk away!" I'm nervous and angry all at the same time. I can't believe this is happening right now.

"You better listen to her bruh and walk away. You don't want none of this." Jason says as he moves around me and closer to Jonathan.

I could tell that Jonathan was about to say something else because his mouth opened, but before anything could come out Shayna grabs him on the shoulder.

"I know you not fighting over this trick. Did you forget you're my boyfriend now?"

We all stood there for a minute looking at each other. Shayna did have a point. I have no idea why Jonathan is so concerned about who I'm seeing. He didn't have a concern when he thought I was pregnant or since he and Shayna have been together. All I keep wondering is who is going to pop off at the mouth next and if there were going to be any blows thrown.

"Chas, if that's how you want to do this; watch what I do." Jonathan says as he looks at me and then looks Jason up and down.

"You made the right choice, bruh." Jason chimes in before Jonathan completely walks away. Jonathan looks back at both of us, but turns around once Shayna puts her hand around the back of his neck to pull him the other way.

Jason and I sit down again. We are silent for a minute.

"I'm really sorry about that. We don't go together anymore and I really don't know why he acted like that."

"It's cool. Don't no guy like his girl or even his old girl smiling in another dude's face; I get it. Don't worry about it. As long as you're okay; I'm good."

"I'm good. We better finish up because the bell is about to ring anyway."

Jason and I continue to talk until the bell rings for class. Jason is cute, goes to church and doesn't mind defending my honor. We'll just have to see how this all goes.

Chapter 23 — Monica

I called Patrick earlier to let him know I was going to come by his house. He told me on the phone that his mother and father were going out to dinner and a movie so we would be alone to talk. Being out of school today was extremely boring and I really missed being with Patrick and everyone else.

I also had to make sure I saw Patrick tonight because Chandra texted me earlier at school and called me after school to tell me what this Trena chick was doing with my Patrick. When she told me that she caught Trena kissing Patrick, I knew then I had to take drastic measures. I would handle Trena when I got back to school, but tonight I was going to confront Patrick. There was no way I was going to let him go. He had some explaining to do, but I already knew what I was going to do. It wasn't right, but I just can't imagine being without Patrick.

I ring the doorbell and Patrick lets me in.

"Hey Lady Monica how are you? I missed you." Patrick grabs me and hugs me. He holds me tight for a few minutes. He releases me and then kisses me on my lips.

When we finished kissing I ask, "Is that how you kissed Trena today?"

He exhales before speaking. "Monica, it wasn't even like that. She caught me off guard. You know I don't want her."

"Yeah, but you did want her before me. First she's sending naked pictures and now she's kissing you behind my back and you let her."

"Monica, you got to believe me. I didn't ask her to send those pictures; she did it on her own. And, I wasn't trying to kiss her; she kissed me."

"Yeah, but you didn't do nothing to stop her and you weren't even going to tell me. Chandra had to tell me everything."

"I was going to tell you Monica. You just need to stop tripping because I don't want to be with Trena."

"Yeah, but if she was giving it up I bet you would do it. Wouldn't you?"

"Monica this makes no sense. Why are we going through this? You know I want to be with you."

"You didn't answer my question. If Trena was giving it up and you two were together you would want it wouldn't you?"

"Okay, Monica since you won't let this go. Yes, if Trena and I were together she and I probably would have sex because that's the kind of girl she is." Patrick sits down on the couch in the living room. I remain standing.

As Patrick is answering my last question, I start pulling off my clothes.

"So is this what I got to do to keep you?" I drop my pants and I'm just about to pull down my panties.

Patrick stands up quickly and grabs my arm so I won't pull them down.

"Monica, chill. If you gonna throw it at me I'm not so sure I can resist so if we're going to stick to what we said about waiting, you better keep your clothes on."

"Yeah, but I don't want to lose you Patrick so if I got to give it up, then let's do this." I get closer to Patrick and he grabs me around my waist.

"Monica we are not going to do this."

I kiss him gently and then it gets intense. He doesn't resist and continues to kiss me. We stop for a minute; just enough time for me to lean back and grab my shirt to lift it up over my head. Patrick releases me slowly.

"Monica, chill!" Patrick yells.

"Don't you want me Patrick?" By now I'm standing in my bra and panties.

"Yes, Monica I do."

I get closer to him once more and start to kiss him again. He goes along with it and then he pushes me away from him.

"What's wrong, Patrick? Isn't this what you want?"

"Monica, put your clothes on." Patrick demands.

"Why?"

"Because we said we were going to be abstinent. And if I keep looking at you like this, I might forget about what we promised each other. So before I attack you, get your clothes on before we regret what happens."

"But I don't want you messing with Trena."

"I'm not, Monica! Get your clothes on. If you don't get those clothes on in sixty seconds, it's going down." Patrick smiles.

I quickly put my clothes back on because I really don't want to have sex with Patrick; at least not now. As I'm putting my clothes back on I can't help, but think how good he is to me. We're both trying to live a Christian lifestyle as teenagers and it's been tough sometimes, but we help each other out when the other gets weak. I almost slipped, but I'm so glad Patrick had my back tonight. I can't let Trena get the best of me either. Things are going to be different when I get back to school.

Chapter 24 – Myra

My mother keeps telling me that she's going to go back to church, but she hasn't been since the last visit. I'm not about to hold my breath, but I really hope she changes her mind. We got another concert coming up so maybe she will come when that happens.

We're going to have a small private session with First Lady Rice because we're doing a special concert for the church anniversary. Pastor selected our group to be the lead group in the concert. There will be other groups performing, but we will be the special guest.

I know when First Lady sees us she's going to have more to share with us than about the concert. We got so much drama going on right now, I'm sure she's going to pick it up in the spirit as she always does.

I walk into the foyer of the church and I don't see anyone so I just take a seat. I guess everyone is running a little late. I grab my phone and start looking through my social media sites. My phone chimes to indicate that I have a text message. I open it up and it's from Xavier.

"Hey Myra what you doing?"

I text back, *"At church. Waiting for First Lady and my friends so we can practice."*

"I miss you."

I text back a smiley face.

"Can't wait to kiss your lips again."

I pause for a minute. I don't know what's up with Xavier, but lately it seems like he wants more than a few kisses on the lips.

I text back another smiley face.

"You know you want to kiss me Myra.....and a whole lot more.

I text back. *"Boy, bye!"*

No sooner than I hit the send button for the text, First Lady Rice walks in the foyer.

"Good morning Myra. How are you sweetheart?" She asks as she walks over to me and gives me a hug.

"I'm good, First Lady. How are you?" I say as I step back and put my phone in my purse. Xavier will just have to wait until I'm finished with this meeting before I respond to anymore of his messages. He just needs to chill. I like him, but I'm not about to make no crazy mistakes; especially about sex. Getting through that drama with Larry and Leroy is really enough to last a lifetime.

"I'm doing great, Myra. The Lord is good and I'm so excited about meeting with you ladies to get ready for this big annual concert for the church anniversary. I know you girls are going to do a great job."

First Lady Rice walks over to one of the big high-back royal blue chairs and takes a seat. She crosses her legs and places her chocolate brown pocketbook on her lap. She pulls out her cell phone and begins texting someone.

Once I saw that she was done texting I respond back to her, "Yes ma'am, we are all excited about this."

"Great. Where are the other girls? Are they all still coming?"

"Yes ma'am. I'm sure they are on their way. I'll call them and see how close they are."

"Okay that will be great. I'm going to my office for a few minutes to get some things organized. When they get here just come into my office and we'll get started."

"Yes ma'am."

As soon as First Lady Rice is out of sight, I pull my cell phone out of my purse and I call Chastity to see where she is.

"Hey, Chas where are you? Are you close by the church yet?"

"Yeah, I'm about two minutes away."

"Okay because First Lady Rice is already here and she's wondering where everyone else is. I'm the only one here so far."

"Oh okay, I'll be there in just a minute. I don't know where everyone else is, but I know I talked with Chandra earlier and she said she was coming. I haven't heard from Monica." Chasity replies.

"Okay, well I'll give Monica a call after I hang up with you."

"Okay I'll see you in a few." Chasity says just before she hangs up with me.

I call Monica and she says she's right outside in the parking lot and she has Chandra with her. I decide to stay in the foyer until they all get there so we can all go in to see First Lady Rice at the same time.

"Hey Myra!" Chandra says while trying to push Monica into the foyer area. Monica waves, but doesn't say a word. She sits down in one of the chairs and just starts starring at one of the pictures on the wall that has a scripture on it. Still no words.

"Hey Chandra." I say while still looking over at Monica to see what's up with her. She isn't saying much, which isn't like her at all.

"Where is First Lady?" Chandra asks.

"She's in her office waiting for us. I figure we wait until Chastity gets here before we go to her office. She's excited about the concert."

"That's cool. I'm excited too."

"So, what's up with you, Monica?" I finally ask since nobody was saying anything about Monica's quietness.

Monica is shaken out of her stare. "I'm good."

"Oh really?" Chandra asks while rolling her eyes upward.

"What is going on?" I ask. I can't stand this suspense in trying to figure out what is going on with Monica.

"She's all upset about this whole thing with Patrick and Trena Lewis. She still can't get over the fact about how Trena sent those pictures to Patrick." Chandra blurts out.

"So that's why we getting the silent treatment? Monica, you can't let that bother you like that anymore." I respond as Chastity walks into the foyer.

"Silent treatment? Who is giving who silent treatment?" Chastity asks while walking towards the other chair. She flops down in the chair.

"Monica is upset about Patrick still."

Monica jumps up and says, "It's not just all about Patrick and Trena. I'm mad at myself too because I just……" Monica stops talking as she recognizes that First Lady Rice is walking up next to her.

"What's going on Monica? Why are you so mad at yourself?" First Lady Rice asks.

Monica pauses and remains silent for a while and so do we all. We all continue sitting in our chairs waiting for Monica to respond. The silence continues as if it is forever.

"It's Patrick….." Monica trails.

"Oh boy here we go." Chandra chimes in.

"Okay this sounds like we need to have a talk in my office before we begin talking about this concert." First Lady Rice shares.

"I think you're right, First Lady Rice." I respond.

"Okay, ladies lets go to my office." First Lady Rice walks towards her office and we all follow after her. Monica is last in line and the last person to walk into First Lady Rice's office. We all wait for her to take a seat.

111

While we're in First Lady Rice's office, we all remain silent. You could hear a pin drop. It seems like hours, but I'm sure it's only been a couple of minutes. Instead of us talking about the concert or preparing to rehearse we're going to take this time to hear what Monica has to get off her chest. We are still sitting, but nobody is saying anything. First Lady Rice finally breaks the silence.

"Okay now that we are here in private girls, fill me in on what is going on with you all. Monica, I know everyone says you have something to share so go ahead and begin, sweetheart."

Monica takes in a deep breath. "First Lady, you know my boyfriend, Patrick?"

"Yes, I remember him."

"Well, he's my soul mate."

"Oh Lord, here we go again with this. Monica, just get to the main point." Chastity says.

"Well, he is my soul mate whether you all believe it or not!" Monica snaps back.

First Lady Rice holds her hand up in front of Chastity and Monica to keep them quiet. "Girls, let's not get into an argument. Remember we are our sister's keeper and we should be able to share what's on our minds without being criticized. So, please let's hear what Monica has to share. Go ahead Monica."

"Like I was saying Patrick is my soul mate, but lately this girl keeps trying to come in between us. Her name is Trena Lewis and she's calling me names, threatening to take my boyfriend away from me and now she had the nerve to send naked pictures of herself to Patrick." Monica exhales after saying all that.

Chandra jumps in before First Lady Rice can say anything else. "She forgot to tell you that she was about to punch Trena Lewis in the face for teasing her. Mrs. Porter had to suspend her for two days out of school because of it."

First Lady Rice frowns at first and then looks at Monica. "Is this true Monica? Did you try to fight another girl because she was calling you names?"

"Yes ma'am." Monica says while looking down at the carpet.

"Monica you know that wasn't the right way to handle that, right?" First Lady Rice asks.

"Yes ma'am, but she got a lot of nerve threatening to take Patrick away from me and for sending him those naked pictures. That wasn't right either." Monica says while sitting at the edge of her seat.

"Yeah but you can't let Trena Lewis have you acting all crazy either Monica. You're out of school and she was still able to stay in school." I say before First Lady Rice can respond back to Monica. She got to understand that she just can't go swinging on people because they do something she doesn't like.

"Monica, you will have to learn to practice as much self-control as possible. I know it may be hard, but if you allow this young lady to get you so upset each time, she will have control over you. She knows exactly what to do to push your buttons, which causes you to react. You see when someone can move you that easily, then you've given them the power to do so. However, you need to know that you have the power to control you. You have the ability to make the right choice. So keep in mind of the kind of outcome you want before you make a choice. You are too beautiful to allow this young lady to move you like that. If Patrick cares about you the way that you care about him, then I'm sure you have nothing to worry about. You got plenty of time to consider who your soul mate is." First Lady smiles at Monica.

"Yes, tell her! We've been trying to get it through her head that she got plenty of time to get serious with someone. Shoot, we only in high school." Chandra says.

"Thank you First Lady Rice for listening. And ya'll just don't understand it now, but Patrick and I are going to get married one day. Just you wait and see."

We all start laughing.

"Girls, now let's not tease Monica. Monica, I think there was something else you wanted to tell me, didn't you? I believe you mentioned that you were mad at yourself for something. Was it because you wanted to punch Trena or was it something else?"

Monica pauses. She sits there and says nothing. She looks at First Lady Rice and then looks at us and then looks back at First Lady Rice. By the look on her face, it was as if she was afraid to share her original point. I wasn't sure what Monica was hiding, but I really wish she would go ahead and share it so we can go over the concert material.

"Monica are you going to say something or what?" Chandra breaks the silence once again.

"I'm embarrassed." Monica lets out after a few more moments of silence.

"Do you want to share this with me in private, Monica?" First Lady Rice asks while reaching out her hand to touch Monica on the shoulder.

"No ma'am. I can share it with my girls too. I just know I'm going to hear it." Monica takes a deep breath again; in and out and then she shares.

"I'm mad with myself because I thought Patrick really wanted Trena after she sent those pictures so I went over to Patrick's house and I started taking my clothes off."

The whole entire room was filled with gasps. I don't think any of us could believe what we were hearing. Out of all of us we all knew Monica and Patrick were adamant about not having sex until they got married. Monica is the main one always encouraging us to remain abstinent. Even after my situation with Larry and Chastity's issue with Jonathan, she always kept telling us we better wait and she wanted us all to make a pack to stay abstinent. So, I think we are all in shock to hear what just came out of Monica's mouth.

"Okay, Monica so after you did that what else happened? Did you have sex with him, Monica?" First Lady Rice asks so calmly.

"No ma'am. We didn't have sex. Patrick told me I better put my clothes on if we were going to continue to practice abstinence."

"Well, thank the Lord for that! Thank God Patrick was strong enough to practice self-control and to respect you enough to not to allow you to slip up. I'm really impressed with Patrick, but very surprised at you Monica. What made you want to do that?" First Lady Rice asks.

"I really didn't want to have sex with Patrick because I know I said we would be abstinent, but because Trena Lewis was coming at him so strong I figured I needed to do something to keep him attracted to me."

"Monica, I understand your thought process, but that is the issue with so many girls. They feel as though they have to give it up in order to keep some boy interested in them. If a boy causes you to stoop below your standards, he's not worth keeping. As the female, you set the standards and they will only go as far as you allow them to." First Lady Rice shares.

"Yes ma'am. I don't know what I was thinking. I mean I just didn't want this girl to take Patrick away from me. I just got caught up."

"Girl, I'm glad Patrick stood his ground. I got to dap him up for that. Talk about practicing self-control to the tenth power....for real." Chandra adds.

"Yes, I'm glad Patrick didn't follow you up Monica. Next time, I don't want you to even take off one piece of clothing in front of Patrick. The old people will say, 'God will keep you if you want to be kept.' It's an old saying, but it is so true. I know sometimes your flesh may get weak, but remind yourself that you've made a commitment to wait." First Lady Rice says as she places her hand on Monica's shoulder.

"Yes ma'am. I'm not going to let that happen again and I'm really glad Patrick shut me down." Monica laughs.

"I know that's right. Kudos to Patrick! Jonathan needs to take some pointers from him." Chastity laughs.

"You are so right about that." I respond.

"Well, girls since we got all that out, let's get some practicing in for this concert. Unless, somebody else has something to discuss." First Lady Rice looks around at all of us to be sure.

"No ma'am." We all chime in.

"Okay, well let's go over the format for the concert and let me hear a few lines of the songs you all are going to sing."

I'm so glad for these talks with First Lady Rice because she knows how to keep us all on track. I just hope Monica doesn't let

Trena Lewis trip her up again. We'll just have to see what happens when she goes back to school. I'm praying now.

Chapter 25 – Chastity

"OMG Chas!!! OMG Chas!!! I can't believe this. OMG! How could he do this to you?"

"Monica, calm down. Breathe, girl. What are you talking about?"

"OMG Chas, you don't know? This is terrible!"

"Monica, I don't know what in the world you are talking about, but I wish you would calm down and tell me what you are talking about."

"Okay, okay! Jesus take the wheel for real."

"Yes, please so He can calm you down." I say as I'm pacing the floor anxious to hear what in the world Monica is talking about.

Before Monica can get out her next sentence, my phone beeps to let me know I have another call coming in. I glance at my screen and it's Chandra."

"Hold on for a minute Monica. Chandra is calling me. Maybe you'll be calm and ready to talk when I get back to the phone."

"Okay, but hurry up Chas because you got to see this."

"Okay, okay. Hold on." I switch over to the other line where Chandra is waiting on me.

"Hello."

"Chas, did you see it? I can't believe this. Why would Jonathan do this?" Chandra screams like I'm a million miles away from her.

"Chandra what are you talking about? You and Monica are saying the same thing, but no one is telling me what is going on!" I scream back.

I can hear the other line on my phone hang up so I'm guessing Monica couldn't wait any longer.

"Hold up Chastity that's Monica beeping in. I'm going to tell her we'll call her back on the three-way." Chandra goes away from the phone for a minute and returns back.

"Okay, I'm back."

"Chandra what is going on?" I'm pacing the floor back and forth because I still don't understand what has Chandra and Monica so worked up.

"Hold up let me add Monica in on the call."

Monica jumps on the call and starts screaming. "I can't believe Jonathan Berry!"

"What happened? What did he do? One of you please tell me what is going on. I can't take this anymore. This is too much! Tell me."

"Chastity are you near your laptop or either check your phone and look at our group chat page. You are not going to believe this." Chandra shares.

"Just tell me!" I yell back.

"No Chastity you got to see this for yourself." Chandra quickly responds.

I open up my laptop, log in and go to our social media group chat. I click on the latest post and when I do, I drop the phone out of my hand.

"Oh my goodness! How could he do this?"

I can hear Chandra and Monica calling me from my cell phone, but for some reason I simply can't move because I can't believe what I'm seeing on this screen. I slowly pick up my phone as I look through all five of these pictures posted on our chat group by Jonathan. And then when I get to the last picture I noticed that the sixth picture isn't a picture, but a video.

I scream out. "I can't believe he did this! This is so messed up!"

"This ain't right. How was he able to do that?" Chandra asks.

"I really don't know how he did that. I mean I know he had his phone with him and he was playing around with it, but he said he wasn't doing anything with it."

"Then he got a nerve to have a short video of all the noise and I think I see some of your body…..yuck!!! Monica lets out.

"Okay. Wait….so if he had his phone, did you let him take pictures or what?" Chandra asks.

There was silence for a few seconds, but I know it felt like a whole lot of minutes to all of us. I know it did for me. I didn't know what to say. I mean I knew Jonathan had his phone and he was teasing about taking pictures and stuff, but I could have sworn he deleted them. I can remember laying down his phone, but he must have pressed record when I got up for a minute to go in the restroom.

"Chastity!" Chandra and Monica scream.

"I didn't know he was actually going to do that. I mean he was playing with the phone at first and then said he was going to take pictures and keep them. I told him to erase them, but I guess he didn't. And he must have set up that video to play after I came back from using the restroom. This is terrible."

"Chas you know everyone in our group is going to see this. If you look at it, it already has two hundred people that have seen it and you can't even delete it. You got to call Jonathan now and tell him to delete it." Monica says.

"I just can't believe he did this. I mean I know he kept saying that he was going to do something if I didn't take him back, but I had no idea it would be this. I thought he was thinking about doing something crazy to hurt himself. I had no idea he would do this." I share while I'm still looking at this madness on the screen. Everybody is starting to view it and now comments are being posted as we speak.

"You got to call him Chas. He got to erase this. Everybody in school is going to be talking about it tomorrow. If you don't set him straight, I will." Chandra says as if she's somebody's mama.

"I know that's right and I'll be right there with you on that Chandra. And you already know Myra don't play either. He can't just do our girl like that and get away with it. He's trying to make

124

you a porn star like Trena Lewis. We can't have that." Monica says and then lets out a loud laugh.

Her laughter eases my tension slightly. We talk for a few more minutes before getting off the phone with each other. As I hang up the phone I fall to my knees and just cry. Tears were coming now, but tomorrow Jonathan Berry may very well feel my fist in his mouth.

Chapter 26 – Chandra

I'm chilling in my room looking at the TV and flicking through the channels. I'm not really looking at anything in particular because I still can't get over this thing with Chastity and Jonathan. I'm still in shock about the whole thing. This is so embarrassing and now everybody in our chat group is going to see it. And if all the people in our group sees it, the whole school is going to know about it eventually. Gossip travels fast at Midland Central. Tomorrow is going to tell it all.

Shortly after we finished talking, I looked at the group again and I noticed that so many people have made comments. A lot of people were saying how disgusting it was.

I'm looking at the group chat now and I see some negative comments about Chastity. It's saying how stupid she is for letting Jonathan take pictures of them. Then as I scroll down, I see some crazy comments from guys giving Jonathan his props for getting that. They're giving him all this praise as if he is some well-known celebrity.

Then I see some stuff that gets me real heated. There are some boys saying they want to get with Chastity since she's giving it up. This whole thing is just going to spoil her reputation. Just when she's trying to do what's right, here comes her past mistakes coming back to haunt her. See that's why I'm not about to give up my panties to no dude. I don't care how much I like them or they like me. I'm not about to let nobody disrespect me like that.

My cell phone rings loudly. It almost scares me. I forgot I had the ringer so high from listening to that video that Jonathan posted. It's Brian calling me.

"Hey Brian."

"Hey Chandra. What are you doing?"

"I'm just sitting here looking at the television?"

"Oh okay. I'm surprised you didn't call me yet."

"What do you mean? Was I supposed to call you? Did we have something planned that I forgot about?"

"Naw, I just looked at the pictures that Jonathan posted in the group with him and Chastity and I thought you would have called to tell me about it." Brian shares.

"Oh yeah, that is a hot mess. I just got off the phone with Chastity and Monica trying to figure all this out. I totally forgot that you were in the chat group. I'm like in total shock right now so I guess it slipped my mind to call you. I just can't believe Jonathan would do that to Chastity."

"Yeah, he probably did it because everybody is saying Chastity wouldn't get back with him so he was going to put it out there to embarrass her."

"Well, he sure did embarrass her. That ain't right. If she didn't want him back, he should have left it alone. He already got him another girl anyway so I don't know why he got to do that to Chas."

"Yeah, he got a new girl, but he really wanted Chastity back and since she didn't want him, I guess he started trippin' and wanted to get her back."

"That is so dumb because now he'll probably never get her back."

"I guess you right, but at least he got that." Brian laughs a little.

I pause for about sixty seconds. I take a deep breath and then I let Brian get an earful.

"What do you mean at least he got it? What is up with you boys? It seems like all you want is to have sex with every girl you meet. What's up with that?"

"That's not really true. Well, for some guys, but not every guy is like that. Some guys just want to get it from the only girl they got."

"Hold up. Flag on the play, Brian. So what are you trying to say?" I already had a feeling where this conversation was going, but I wanted to see how all this was going to play out.

"Any guy who got a girlfriend at some point wants to take the relationship a little further than just kissing and holding hands. He want to show her how much he cares by doing more than that."

Oh boy. Brian must really think I'm a fool. I hope he don't think I'm about to give it up. I don't care if we do go together. I ain't about to lower my standards for nobody. I'm not about to get tripped up like Chas' and be worried about getting pregnant or getting my naked pictures posted in a group chat. Nope. It's not going to happen.

"Brian, what are you really trying to say?"

"Alright Chandra if you really want to know the truth I think it's time you and I did that."

"Brian, I'm not about that and I'm not about to start it now."

"Come on Chandra. Give me a chance to make you feel good. I'm not going to hurt you or get you pregnant."

"Oh yeah, how do you know that? Too many sperm cells be running all around. You can't stop all of them." I ask as I stand up and start pacing around the room. This conversation is getting serious.

"I'll wear a condom, Chandra."

"No, Brian. I'm not ready for that."

"Well, when you going to be ready?"

"When I get married!" I yell back. I know that will shut him down. He is silent and it seems hours have passed before he finally says something.

"I can see we aren't going to get anywhere with this tonight. I'll bring it up again. Anyway, I was calling to ask you to come to a get together at a friend's house. It will be just a few of us hanging out."

"Oh yeah, who?"

"One of the football players; you don't know him. We just all getting together with our girls for end of season party. I want you to come."

"Okay, I'll go with you, Brian."

"That's my girl. Its next week so we'll talk about it before then. I guess I'll let you go for tonight and I'll see you tomorrow in school."

"Alright, Brian. I'll chat with you tomorrow. Good night."

I really don't know how much longer I can keep telling Brian no to having sex, but I'm willing to keep telling him until he stops asking. I just wonder how long that will be.

Chapter 27 – Myra

My mother is about to go on a date with her new friend. I haven't really meant him personally because every time she goes out with him she doesn't invite him in. I knew something was going on because lately she's been talking on the phone late at night. When she would walk around the house with the phone glued to her ear she would be smiling and giggling like she's my age. She's walking around here acting like she's a teenager in love with a new boo. I just hope for her sake and ours that he's not some crazy nut like Leroy.

The latest news we heard about Leroy is that he got hooked up with this other lady who had a daughter and he actually did sexually assault her. I was really saddened by the news because nobody should have to go through that. I mean nobody; not even my worst enemy. I couldn't help but think that her story could have been my story had I not spoken up. Even though my mother didn't believe me at first, I was glad we caught him in time.

"Myra, come in the living room for a minute." My mom calls me from downstairs.

"Yes ma'am. I'll be right there." I put my book down that I was reading and walk out of my room to go downstairs to my mother.

I finally get downstairs and I look at my mother and she is all dressed up and her make up is flawless. I sit down next to her on the couch to hear what she has to say.

"Myra, I got a date tonight with someone I've been seeing for a couple of weeks now and I wanted you to meet him. He's really nice and he has money!!!" My mom's eyes lit up like a Christmas tree when she mentions he has money. I chuckle a little.

"Okay well what does he do?" I ask.

"He's a building contractor and he owns some rental properties too." As my mother speaks I can see a sparkle in her eyes.

"Oh, that's cool. So is he nice to you?" I ask.

"Yes so far so good. I haven't told him about you and Michael yet so he really doesn't know that I have children." My mother says as she looks down at the carpet.

I turn my head to the side as if I'm confused. "You haven't told him about us and you've been dating him for a couple of weeks? Why did you do that?"

My mother takes in a deep breath and then releases it. "I don't know Myra. I just want someone in my life for me. I didn't want to mention it until I was sure he was a good person to be with and to be around my kids."

I hear what my mother is saying, but I really wish she wouldn't get so caught up with these men. I don't know if I really like the fact that she didn't tell this guy about me and my brother. I mean to me, it seems like she's living a lie. I'm just wondering what will happen when she finally does tell him about us.

"Listen, Myra I called you down here because I wanted you to meet him. He's coming to pick me up and I wanted to introduce him to you."

"Okay. I hope he's cool." I say as I grab a magazine off of the coffee table.

"I'm sure you're going to like him. He has enough money to take care of all of us and them some." My mom grins again from ear-to-ear.

The doorbell rings and my mother jumps up like she's a fresh bag of new popped popcorn. She runs to the door like she's running a marathon race. I laugh a little. This is going to be interesting.

She finally opens the door after a long pause. She stares at him for a minute. He stares back.

"Are you going to let me in or what?" He asks.

"Sure, I want to let you in, but I have something to share with you." My mother adds as she allows him to walk in the house.

They walk around to where I am sitting and he looks at me and I look at him. He doesn't look all that to me. She must be attracted to his money.

"Who is this? Your niece?" He asks.

"No, Robert. This is not my niece. Have a seat. I want to share something with you."

I remain silent because I'm not so sure how this conversation is going to go or how it is going to end. He finally sits down next to my mother on the couch and I'm sitting alone on the chair near the couch.

"Robert, I want you to meet my daughter, Myra."

"Your daughter? You never told me you had a daughter or kids for that matter."

"I know I didn't, but I wanted to be sure things were good with us before I told you. I also have a son too who is eleven years old. He's not here right now because he's at basketball practice."

"So you have a son and a daughter?"

"Yes."

Silence fills the room. You could probably hear a pin drop on the carpet. Not sure what this guy is thinking about, but he better say something quick before my mother starts panicking.

"Patricia, I had no idea you had children. Why didn't you tell me earlier? I mean, why did you keep this from me? I don't like it when a woman plays games."

"I'm not playing games with you Robert. I just didn't want to share about my children until I knew things were good with us."

"Good with us? I don't understand that Patricia. This doesn't set right with me because if you have been keeping your children away from me who's to say what else you will keep from me. I mean it sounds like you've been lying."

Okay, this isn't really going how my mother anticipated; I'm sure. I'm just going to sit here and see how all this pans out.

"Robert, I haven't been lying to you. I just didn't want to tell you about my children until I was sure we were going to keep dating. I mean my kids and I have been through a lot in my previous relationships and I didn't want to expose them to the wrong kind of person."

My mother sounds like she's begging this guy to understand. I mean I get his point because she should have said something about us. She didn't have to let him meet us until she was sure, but to say absolutely nothing about having children is a bit over the top.

"I can't help what another man did to you. I'm not that guy, but what I don't like is to be lied to or someone to be deceptive. I don't have time for games, Patricia."

"I'm not playing games, Robert." My mother repeats and looking into the eyes of this guy as if she's a child that has lost her way and she's begging for someone to take her home.

He takes a deep breath. "You know what? Maybe it's best that you and I just be friends. I can't deal with this news about you having children. I really wasn't looking to get involved with anyone with children if possible. And if I was, I would have preferred if she told me upfront. I can't deal with someone who is deceptive anyway." He says as he's turning away from my mother and heading towards the front door.

"Wait a minute, Robert!" My mother yells out as she grabs his arm.

"Patricia, I can't do this."

"I don't understand. I mean I know I should have told you about the children, but I'm not the type of woman you're describing. I thought we had a good vibe."

"I thought so too, but I'm not trying to be with a woman who is looking for a meal ticket for her kids. I'm not taking care of nobody else's kids. The last girl I dated knew I had money and she just wanted to use me to take care of her and her children. I'm not about that life." He keeps walking towards the door.

"Robert, I can't believe this. I'm not that woman." My mother pleads.

There is a whole lot of begging going on in this room and I'm not even liking this whole conversation at all. I really can't believe that I'm still sitting here. Who does this guy think he is anyway? He must think he's a gift to all women who are single parents. Boy, bye. Help my mother to open her eyes.

"Get somebody else to take care you and your children. It was nice meeting you, but I got a feeling this is not going to go well. Take care, Patricia." Robert opens the door and walks out without giving my mother a chance to say another word.

My mother hits on the door like she's hitting on a punching bag. "I can't believe this. I just can't believe this." She yells as she turns around and leans against the door.

I stand up and then walk over towards her. As I do, I see some tears rolling down her eyes. She's saying she can't believe this, but I'm feeling the same way. I can't believe she is actually crying over this dude who just said he didn't want to be with anyone with children. Boy, bye for real.

"Ma, don't cry." I grab my mother and hug.

"It's not fair, Myra." She says as she wipes her eyes with her hand.

"What's not fair, Ma?"

"Him dumping me because I didn't tell him about my children? Really? Who does that?"

Obviously he does; I was thinking, but I knew I shouldn't say it out of my mouth because apparently my mother feels like she's lost her soul mate or something.

"Ma, if he feels like that he probably wasn't worth it any way." I finally say after a moment of silence.

"I just don't understand why I can't get a decent man in my life. I mean, Robert was a good man and he had a lot of money. He could take care of all of us, but I don't understand why he made such a big deal just now."

"Ma, why are you so worried about getting a man?"

"Myra, I'm tired of being alone!" My mother says as she storms out of the living room and runs upstairs.

I hear her bedroom door slam. This whole thing really sounds crazy to me. I really wish my mother would just get over the thought of getting a man in her life. I want to tell her to just chill especially after all the drama that Leroy took us through. Somebody needs to talk to her. I'm going to put my mother on my prayer list.....for real.

Chapter 28 — Monica

I've decided that I'm not going to let myself get so worked up about Trena Lewis. I'm not about to let her get me kicked out of school again. I can't afford to miss classes. I have so much more to offer Patrick; literally, so I'm not about to let her frustrate me anymore. I got this. At least that's what I'm telling myself while looking at my bathroom mirror. I'm giving myself a motivational pep talk before I leave out for school. I think it's working. I just hope it lasts when I face Patrick and Trena Lewis.

"Monica, are you coming out of that bathroom or what? You're going to be late for school if you don't hurry up!" My mother yells from downstairs.

I look in the mirror one more time. My outfit looks good. I look good and I'm not about to let Trena Lewis get me down.

"Okay I'm coming now, Ma." I yell back while grabbing my pocketbook and my book bag.

I get downstairs and my mother is standing by the door that's in the kitchen, which leads to our garage. She smiles at me.

"Now don't you let any of those girls or Patrick take you off track today, Monica. You don't have any time to waste on that drama. You have too many great things ahead of you to let anything or anybody block it."

"Yes ma'am. You're right."

My mom grabs my hand and says a short prayer before we leave out the door. I hope Patrick got Trena straight while I was gone because I just want to enjoy my day.

As soon as I get into school, I see Patrick walking down the hallway. He waves at me and I wave back. He starts running towards me. When he finally catches up to me he gives me a tight hug and then kisses me on my lips.

"Hey you two watch that PDA!" Mrs. Porter yells out. She's standing outside her classroom in the hallway while everyone is trying to get to class.

"Okay, Mrs. Porter." I say and start laughing.

"Welcome back, Monica." She yells back.

"Thank you." I say and then I look at Patrick.

Patrick grabs my hand, looks into my eyes and smiles this goofy smile like he's in love with me. I smile back.

"How's my Lady Monica?"

"I'm good. And you?"

"I'm real good now. You not still mad at me are you?"

"No, not really. I guess I can forgive you."

"Good because I never told her to send those pictures to me in the first place."

"Did you erase them?" I ask.

"Yes, I did erase them. I told you I don't want Trena. I love my chocolate girl." Patrick smiles and then gives me another quick kiss on the lips before Mrs. Porter could see.

If you could see me blush through my dark skin, I would be completely red all over even down to my big toe.

"Okay, if you say so, Patrick."

"Yes, I say so." Patrick puts his arm around my waist.

"Well, we better get to class. I know Mrs. Porter is still probably checking us out. I have her this period."

"Yeah, you know Mrs. Porter be on the lookout." Patrick laughs and I laugh with him.

As I get ready to turn to go to Mrs. Porter's class, I see a group of girls in my peripheral vision. And then I hear them laughing and I think they are pointing at someone.

"Don't nobody like no burnt meat." Trena says loudly while walking towards me and Patrick.

I know she's not talking about me. At least I hope she's not talking about me because I'm not in the mood for Trena Lewis. I take a deep breath.

"Don't you say a word, Monica. I'll handle this." Patrick says as he stands in front of me.

Trena and two of her friends come right up to us. I'm not feeling this at all.

"What's up Trena?" Patrick asks.

"You are what's up Patrick. I still don't see why you want this burnt meat." She says as she looks over at me.

My heart is pumping fast and my hands curl into fists. I know I'm supposed to remain calm, but this girl is a bit too much.

"Listen, Trena you better stop talking about my girl. I already told you I don't want anything to do with you."

"I don't see why not. I can't believe you going to pass this up for that piece of black charcoal." The girls around her laugh.

"Well, this black charcoal, burnt meat must taste real good to him because he's not leaving it for you." I say while leaning closer to Patrick.

Trena places her hand on her hips and rolls her neck and she speaks. "Girl, he's just saying that in front of you. That's not what he was saying while you was out."

"Stop lying, Trena. What part of I don't want to be with you don't you understand?"

"Patrick you have lost your mind." Trena responds.

"Trena even if I didn't have Monica I wouldn't want a girl like you anyway because you don't respect yourself so I know you wouldn't respect me. See girls like you think the only thing a guy wants from you is your body so you think that's all you got to offer. Everybody ain't like that and I'm one of them. So I just need you to back off from me and my girl."

"So what are you gay or something?" Trena says as she tilts her head to the side. The girls with her chuckle.

"No, I'm a Christian and I don't want to mess around with a girl who is so quick to give it up, but you wouldn't understand

144

that. You probably got a disease and don't know it yet. You better check yourself."

Patrick turns to me, puts his arm around my shoulders and we start walking away towards Mrs. Porter's class.

I'm smiling because I know Trena got her mouth wide open. She doesn't have a clue. She needs to realize that not every boy wants to see her nasty pictures on their phone. I love it when Patrick stands up for me and stands up for God.

Chapter 29 – Chastity

I dread the thought of going to school today that's why I'm still in the bed. I told my mother I was sick and my stomach was upset so I needed to lay down a little longer. Not sure how long she's going to let me lie here, but I may need to hold out as long as I can because I really don't want to face Jonathan.

"Chastity Renee Robertson, you better get out of that bed so you can get to school. You're not about to cut school today so roll out of that bed and get in the shower." My mother says from down the hall from her bedroom.

I hate it when she calls my whole name. It makes me feel like I'm in trouble for something. I really don't want to go. I haven't told my father or mother anything yet, but I got a feeling I'm going to need to. This whole thing makes me want to just crawl under a rock.

I sit up in the bed and place my feet on the floor. I sit there in that same position for at least another ten minutes. Trying to decide whether to get dressed or lay back down in the bed.

I hear a knock on my door, which causes me to slightly jump. It's my mother. She peeks her head in the room.

"Chastity, why are you still in the bed?" She says as she walks over to me.

"I'm just not feeling it at all today, Mom." I respond, but before I finish the sentence a few tears cascade down my cheek.

"Chastity, what is wrong, baby? Why are you crying?" My mother says as she sits down next to me and holds me in her arms.

Why did she do that because now the tears start coming down my cheeks faster than they ever had. I don't know what's coming over me, but I guess I got to release this anger. I know now that there is no way I can get out of my room without telling my mother what is going on.

"It's Jonathan." I manage to say through my sniffling. I grab a tissue from out of my tissue box and wipe my eyes and nose.

"Chastity I know you're not crying over Jonathan Berry. Girl, you better forget him and thank God you didn't get pregnant at your age."

"I'm over him, Mom. It's just that....." My sentence fades away.

"It's what? How can I help you Chastity if you don't tell me what's going on."

The only way to solve this is to just get it out because if I don't do it now, my mother is going to keep bugging me all day.

I take a deep breath. Breathe in and breathe out. "When I messed up and had sex with Jonathan, he took pictures of us. I really didn't know he was doing that. He was playing around. So now he's posted those pictures on our social media group. Everyone can see them."

"Oh my goodness, Chastity. That is terrible. Why would Jonathan do such a thing?"

"I don't know. I guess he's mad because I won't take him back. I told him I just want to be friends and that's it. I don't want to fall in that trap again and I definitely don't want to get pregnant now."

"I know that's right. I'm not ready for any grandbabies now. It's best to leave those boys alone when it comes to sex. You and Jonathan are too young to deal with all the emotions that goes along with being sexually active. It's best to just wait until you are married."

"Yes ma'am. I really want to wait until I get married. I don't need that drama in my life. So because I don't want to have sex with Jonathan anymore, he posted these pictures of us to get back at me."

"Jonathan Berry needs a beating. I need to bring my belt to school and beat his behind down the hallway. Somebody needs to take a picture of that and post it." My mother laughs.

I laugh too. The thought of my mother beating Jonathan with a belt down the hallways sounded real crazy, but a part of me wishes she could get away with it.

"I think that would be cool. Although, I know Jonathan wouldn't like it. But what gets me is that Jonathan already has another girlfriend."

"Really? So why is he posting pictures of you and him?" My mother's right eyebrow raises up. It always does that when she is in shock about something or upset.

"That's what I was thinking too. Why would he even bother posting pictures of me and him when he got somebody else he's having sex with?"

"Oh Lord, Jonathan better slow down before he catches the cooties. He better watch it before he catches something he can't wash off with soap and water." My mother laughs again.

"That's what I was thinking too because the girl he's messing around with has been with so many guys at school it's ridiculous. She dresses like she used to standing on a corner."

"That's terrible Chas. You're just going to have to hold your head up and just deal with all the talk because it's nothing you can do about it now. Everyone has seen the pictures, but I'm going to call Jonathan's mother and tell her to have him remove those pictures."

"Okay. I was hoping he would take them down himself, but I looked late last night and they were still there."

"Don't worry. I'll handle that. You just get out of this bed and get in the shower. You got too much work to do at school to be missing over this."

"Yes ma'am." I get up from my bed and get my things ready to take a shower. I know a lot of people are going to have a lot to say, but I guess I'm just going to have to deal with it.

Chapter 30 – Chastity

I take a deep breath before walking in the front doors of Midland Central High. I really don't want to see people whispering as I pass by and I don't want anybody giving me the side-eye or people pointing and laughing at me. I'm definitely not in the mood for that today. I just want to get through this day. I'm hoping that my mom can talk to Jonathan's mother and make him take down the pictures.

As soon as I begin walking down the hallway, I hear someone yelling. "You not going to get my man back!"

I look behind me to see who it is and who they are talking to and lo and behold it's Shayna Jefferson. I try to ignore her because I'm really not sure if she is talking to me, but knowing her she probably is.

"You heard me. Don't act like you don't know who I'm talking to. He's not coming back to you anyway." She continues. Her voice is either getting louder or she's getting closer to me.

She's close to me. Real close. The next thing I feel is a hand on my shoulder.

"Chastity, don't act like you don't hear me talking to you." Shayna says.

I turn around to face her. "I heard you talking, but I didn't know who you were talking to. I don't want your boyfriend….or your man as you call him."

"Then why you put them pictures up on the chat group?"

"I didn't put those pictures up in the chat group. You better check with your man because he is the one who put them up there."

"Now you lying because he said you put them up there." Shayna says as she places her hand on her big hips.

"I'm not the one lying. Jonathan is lying. I never wanted any pictures like that up for everyone to see."

"Girl, please. You know you want everyone to think you can get Jonathan back by showing those pictures. What you not going to do is stand up here and lie like you didn't put them up there."

"Shayna, I don't know what kind of lies that Jonathan has been putting in your head, but I don't want Jonathan back and I didn't put up those pictures. If you look at the post, you'll see who put it up." I say while rolling my eyes. I mean how stupid can she be? Doesn't she know you can see who put the post up? Duh....she needs to pay more attention in school then giving it up to every boy she dates.

"Whatever.....you not getting him back so don't even think about it. Plus, what he's getting now is far better than what you gave him." Shayna says while patting her private area.

I don't mean no harm, but I got to preach to this chic because she has no clue.

"First of all Shayna, I'm not in any competition with you to see who can have sex the best because there is more to life than just having sex with a boy."

Shayna interrupts. "You only saying that because he told you I was better than you." Shayna laughs.

"Girl, you got it twisted. Jonathan don't know what he's doing either. Besides, I got a lot more respect for myself. I know me and Jonathan made a mistake by having sex with each other, but I'm not about to let myself get tripped up like that again. I got better respect for myself and I'm not about to let no boy make me lower my standards."

"I got respect for myself. I got standards too because I be with who I want to be with. Everybody don't get this." Shayna says as she taps her private area with her hand again.

I don't know why this girl thinks her private area is a gold mine or something. She must be stuck on herself because she must not know that a lot of girls got private areas that boys want to get to. Hers is no different. Somebody needs to school her on that, but for now I better get her to understand she needs to respect herself better than what she's doing. All I keep thinking is that she needs to sit in one of our teen sessions with First Lady Rice.

"Shayna, like I said there is more to life than just having sex with a boy. You got to think about your reputation. Too many people are going around saying the only reason a boy wants to be with Shayna Jefferson is because she's giving it up. They don't want you for just you, they know you're going to have sex with them. They got a name for that you know."

"I ain't no hoe!!!" Shayna yells back.

"Yeah, but you got a sign up that says you are. They know it by how you act, what you say and because you giving it up.

After a while Jonathan is going to drop you too because deep inside he knows better. A guy is going to use you up as long as he can, but you not going to be the type he keeps."

"Jonathan ain't going to dump me." Shayna says.

I breathe in and out. I can tell this is going to take more time than I thought to get her to understand it ain't all about sex. She need to slow down before she catches something; if she hasn't already.

"Shayna, let me ask you something. Have you gotten tested for an STD?"

"No, I ain't got no diseases. You tripping."

"How do you know you don't have any? I know Jonathan is not the only boy you been with in Midland Central."

"You need to mind your business. You just better take those pictures down and stay away from Jonathan or you're going to get the beat down."

I don't even know why I'm about to ask her this because she is really getting on my nerves with protecting her and Jonathan's relationship. She doesn't have a clue that after a while Jonathan is going to kick her to the curb. Little does she know, he was only hooking up with her to make me jealous? Sad part for him is; it didn't work.

"Shayna, I don't want Jonathan so you don't have to worry about me, but what you need to get is some respect for yourself. You need to seriously think about coming to one of our teen sessions with our First Lady. She can help you understand a whole lot better about self-respect than I can. Boys at our age are only after one thing and if you're always giving it up, they coming for you. They don't like you for you, they like you because of what you got down there. Come on Shayna, you're *better than that*."

Oh my goodness. What am I saying? I'm sounding like my mother, Mrs. Porter and First Lady Rice all at one time. Never in a million years would I think I would be saying this to another teenage girl, but ain't that like God to put words in your mouth when you really don't want to say nothing.

"Girl, bye!" Shayna says.

"Think about it Shayna. We're having a meeting next Saturday at twelve o' clock noon. You should stop by. It's at New Beginnings Christian Center on Broad Street."

"Whatever…..I might be there." Shayna says as she walks away from me.

I inhale and exhale. I guess I'll just have to wait and see if she shows up, but at least I planted the seed. I really didn't want to plant it at all, but you know how God does stuff sometimes. I'm sure my Mom and First Lady Rice would be proud of me. Now I just got to face Jonathan.

Chapter 31 – Brian

The bell is just about to ring and I'll be glad to get out of this Spanish class. I know they say we need to learn another language, but I'm good with just knowing English. Spanish has too many things to remember.

Finally the bell rings and everyone jumps out of their seats to get out of the class. Dr. Sanchez wasn't even finished with her sentence before we all walked out of there. She didn't say anything this time because I think she could tell we were all ready to get out of class.

I'm walking down the hallway to get to my next class and I see Tyrik coming my way. I really want to turn around because I already know he's going to ask me about Chandra. Really it's none of his business so I don't know why he keeps asking me.

I get what he's saying, but I just got to take it slow with Chandra. She's been saying no, but I think she'll give in if I keep bringing it up.

Tyrik walks up to me and daps me up. "What's up?"

"Nothing, man just chillin'. On my way to this next class."

"Alright, cool. I'm about to head to Spanish class, but I really want to go across the street and smoke on this blunt." Tyrik laughs. His eyes already look watery like he's already had one blunt too many.

I heard Tyrik was into a lot of stuff and some of that stuff was drinking and smoking weed. He's asked me before to smoke with him, but I told him I'm not down with that. I'm an athlete and I'm not about to do anything to mess up this body or mess up any chances to get a scholarship. I just laugh with him or really at him.

"Cool man. You do you. I'm about to get down this hallway before this bell rings." I start to turn away from Tyrik, but then he grabs me on my arm.

"Alright. Hey, did you get that yet?"

Here we go. He wants to know about Chandra. I mean I want to be with Chandra, but she's not feeling that right now. I don't know why Tyrik is so concerned about what I'm doing. I got a feeling I should have never entertained a conversation with him in the first place.

"Naw, man, but I'm good. It's just going to take longer than I thought." I respond.

I really didn't want to have this conversation with Tyrik because I'm a little embarrassed that Chandra and I haven't done anything. Then another part of me really has respect for Chandra so I'm not trying to pressure her too much. The last conversation we had about it, she definitely wasn't down, but I can't let Tyrik think that I'm soft and don't want to get with my girl. Chandra and I are cool, but I wouldn't mind getting with her. Plus Tyrik been going around telling some of the football players that I haven't hit that yet. Everybody keep asking me about it except Patrick.

"How can you be good? You ain't got those panties yet? I told you come by my house for that small house party I'm having and I'll make sure you get one of the bedrooms in the house so you can handle that. Plus, I got some stuff to help you with it. She won't even know what hit her."

"Alright, Tyrik. I already told her about the party. We'll see. I'll talk with you later about it because I'm about to be late for this class." I dap Tyrik and walk down the hallway.

As I'm walking down the hallway I send Chandra a text to remind her about the party. A few seconds before I step into the classroom, Chandra text back to let me know she didn't forget about the party. Not sure how this is going to turn out, but I guess I'm willing to give it a try. I just hope Chandra gives in before then because I'm not so sure about all that Tyrik is talking about.

Chapter 32 — Myra

My mom is working the night shift at the GoTel call center so it's just me and Michael home tonight. I know my mother doesn't like me having company over on a school night, but she said it was okay that Xavier stop by for a little while.

My mom really likes Xavier because he is so unlike Larry. I still can't believe I allowed Larry to be in my life for as long as I did. I'm glad for my friends and for First Lady Rice helping me to understand that I deserve to be treated *better than that*.

Michael is in his room playing some video games. He's been in there since my mother went to work. The way he's in there talking and yelling at the game, I don't think he'll be coming out of there no time soon.

The living room couch feels so good. I got my big blue furry blanket covering me and I feel so comfortable. I got the remote in my hand trying to figure out what to look at until Xavier gets here. As I grab a handful of popcorn, I get a text from Xavier.

Hey, I'm outside. Open the door.

Okay.

I walk over to the door to open it up for Xavier. As soon as he sees me, he grabs me tight and kisses me on the lips.

After a few seconds, I release myself from his hold. I look him in his eyes and just smile. He kisses me again.

"Alright, Xavier Johnson you better chill." I say as I pull him into the house.

"What? Can't I be glad to see my girl? You gonna fuss at a brother for that?" Xavier says while standing over me while I'm sitting on the couch.

I grab him by the arm and pull him down so he can sit with me on the couch.

"Okay, okay Xavier I get it."

"Yeah, I wish I could get it." Xavier says as he leans over and kisses me again.

"Boy what has gotten into you?"

"What do you mean, Myra? I'm a teenage boy and I can't help it if I want to get closer to my girl."

"Yeah, but I don't want you to disrespect me, Xavier."

"I'm not going to disrespect you, but I can't help it if I'm attracted to you, Myra."

"Okay, okay. On another note, what do you want to watch?"

"Whatever you want is fine with me. Where is your brother?" Xavier says while looking around the room.

"Don't worry about him, he won't be coming in here bothering us because he's in his room playing those video games. To try to get him out of there would be like pulling a tree out the ground with your bare hands. He's not budging."

Xavier laughs. "I get the same way sometimes when me and my brother play the basketball video game against each other."

"Ya'll a trip when it comes to those games. I don't get what's the big deal. Anyway, let's look at this movie." I say after flicking through the channels for a while. The movie is a love story about this girl and guy who happen to also like basketball.

"Yeah, this is cool."

While Xavier is relaxing, I get two sodas out of the refrigerator and pop some more popcorn. When I return to the couch, Xavier is all into the movie.

I sit down next to him and hand him a soda. He grabs a handful of popcorn and so do I. Before you know it we're both start hearing the crunching noise from the popcorn in our mouths. The popcorn tastes so good. It has extra butter on it, which is my favorite. It's melting in my mouth. For a while we're sitting quietly looking at the movie.

I feel Xavier's arm go around my shoulder. He leans over and kisses me on the cheek and then my neck. I move my neck a little. He grabs my chin and turns my face to him and then he starts kissing me. I kiss him back. It gets intense. I'm starting to get this tingly feeling all over my body and I'm liking it. Xavier starts moving his hand up my shirt to touch my breasts.

Immediately the thought comes to my mind……*hold up! I can't do this. I got to do better.*

"Xavier, stop."

"Come on Myra. You know you like it." He says as he kisses my lips.

I pull back. "Xavier, cut it out. This ain't good."

163

"I'll make it good." Xavier leans in and starts kissing me again. I'm trying to resist, but his lips against mine feel so good.

His hands are all over me. And then I feel him do something else….my zipper on my jeans is coming down. I feel him trying to climb on me and then the thought comes again. *I got to do better.*

I stop kissing and push Xavier. "Stop Xavier, right now. I'm not doing this."

"Myra, you want it just like I do. Stop playing. You gave it to Larry so it ain't like you a virgin."

No he didn't just say that. I push Xavier off me and he ends up on the floor. I didn't realize my own strength and neither did Xavier. He looks at me like he was just thrown to the floor by the Incredible Hulk.

"Get out Xavier." I stand up.

"Why you tripping, Myra?"

"Xavier you better get out because I'm not about to do this with you and I don't appreciate what you said. You better leave."

"Chill, Myra. I didn't mean to say that. I just got caught up."

"Well, you can take your caught-up self out of here. I'm not about to let anyone disrespect me anymore. You know Larry did me wrong and you got the nerve to bring that up. You acting like him. I ain't having it. You can leave now."

"Myra, come on now. Chill." Xavier grabs my hand.

"Xavier, I'm not about to let you or anyone else try to make me do something I don't want to do. Yeah, I got a little caught up too, but I'm not about to have sex with you. When I was with Larry he made me have sex with him and I'm not about to go down that road for nobody; not even you. Good night, Xavier." I say as I walk towards the front door to let him out.

He follows me to the door. "Look, Myra. I'm sorry, okay?"

"Whatever. I can't do this. I can't believe you. You already know what I went through with Larry. You better leave."

"I thought you would be okay with it."

"Okay with it? I already told you I didn't want to have sex and that I was being abstinent. I might have slipped up before, but I'm not going there no more. I'm a Christian and just like First Lady Rice says, *no sex before marriage*. I'm sticking to the script. Bye Xavier."

Xavier looks at me with sad eyes. He tries to hug me and I push him away. He walks out and I shut the door behind him. He got a lot of nerve thinking he can disrespect me since he knew I allowed Larry to disrespect me for so long. Nope. Not today. No more. Not ever.

Chapter 33 – Chastity

I sent a text to Myra, Monica and Chandra to let them know we were all going to meet up lunch time. I got my food from the cafeteria and of course it's nasty again. I don't understand where they get this food from. It can't be from a real grocery store or food wholesale place. It's got to come from some place where people dump food nobody wants to eat and then they mix it up and serve it to school cafeterias. Then the cafeteria staff be smiling at you while they serve it as if they are serving you a full course meal. They have hospitality, but something seriously has to be done with school cafeteria food. It's not healthy. It's just not safe.

I walk to the table with my food tray in my hands. When I get to the empty table, I can't help but notice that Jonathan and Shayna are sitting about three tables away. I haven't said anything to him yet, but I know it's going to happen soon.

I place my tray down and take my seat. I say my grace over my food and then I sip my grape juice. As I place my juice carton down on the table, I feel a soft tap on my right shoulder.

"Hey Lady." Jason says while smiling with those pretty teeth.

"Hey Jason. How are you?" I say while wrapping my arms around his neck to give him a hug.

"I'm good now that I'm looking at you."

"Thank you, Jason. You going to eat lunch?"

Jason takes a seat next to me. "Yeah, I'm going to eat something; probably the pizza. I remember you telling me that was the safest thing to eat and you are right. That's all I've been eating since we ate together the first time."

"Yup that pizza is the best thing they got going on in this cafeteria. Everything else needs to go to the dogs, well, not even the dogs deserve to be treated like this."

We both laugh. Then Jason looks into my eyes, but not just in my eyes. It feels like he's looking into my soul.

"What is it Jason?" I finally ask after about a minute. It felt like hours though because his look seemed so strong.

"I just like looking at you. You're so pretty. I really wanted to ask you something, but I don't want to interrupt your lunch."

"Go ahead. Ask me. I'm just waiting on my friends to come sit with me. We got to catch up on the latest gossip from each other." I laugh.

Jason smiles back at me. "I don't know if you're ready for this or not, but I really want to spend some more time with you. Would you be down for that?"

I smile at first. What was Jason up to? I mean what does he really mean about spending more time together? Why do boys talk in circles sometimes? Boy, what do you want?

"That would be cool." I finally say.

Jason takes a deep breath and says, "Well, that's not all that I want to ask, but we can talk more about it later." He leans over and gives me a kiss on the cheek.

"Oh, I'm sorry are we interrupting something?" Chandra asks with a big smirk on her face.

"Yeah, should we go to another table, Chas?" Monica asks while grinning from ear-to-ear as if she just won a lump sum of money.

"Don't let us stop you. I mean we just your best friends." Myra says with a grin on her face like she's joking, but you can hear the sarcasm all up in her voice.

"Stop playing.....we are just talking." I respond back to them.

"It's cool. I'll let you sit with your friends. We'll talk about this later. I'll call you tonight." Jason says as she stands up.

"Okay Jason."

Jason walks away and they all start drilling me about my conversation with him.

"Look at her blushing. I think somebody got a new boyfriend." Chandra says after eating some of her French fries.

"Girl, stop. He's so nice, but I don't know if he wants to get with me like that."

"Well, it look that way when we walked up on you two. Kissing and carrying on." Monica says while she's acting like she's blowing kisses at someone.

"Anyway......let's move on to the next person. What's going on with you, Myra?" I say while grabbing my hot dog. I was not ready to be put in the hot seat about Jason because I wasn't so sure where it was going anyway. I know where I would like for it to go, but I don't want to jump the gun. I'll see what he's talking about tonight.

"Okay, so you passing the baton to me? It's all good. I know you want to get out of that hot seat. I got to tell you all about Xavier and what he tried to do when he came by the other night."

"What's up?" Chandra asks.

"Well, he came by and we started kissing and the next thing I know his hands are all over me."

"Myra, please tell me you two didn't have sex." Monica says with that eyebrow raised like she's about to give someone a beat down.

"No, Monica we didn't."

"Good."

"Well what happened?" I ask.

"Chas, he started kissing me and it got a little heated, but then I told him to stop and I said I didn't want to do that. He had the nerve to say that I gave it up to Larry and I know I'm not a virgin so what's the big deal."

"What????!!!" Chandra yells as she throws her piece of pizza down on her tray as if it is the nastiest piece of pizza she's ever eaten.

"No he didn't." Monica says.

"Yes, he did. I couldn't believe him. I told him to get out of my house because I wasn't about to stand for no more disrespect from nobody."

"I know that's right. Did he at least apologize?" I ask as I place my hand on Myra's shoulder.

"Yes, he did, but I'm not jumping back into that again. He's going to have to do a whole lot more than apologize. Larry used to do crazy stuff to me and say some mean things and then he would apologize. As soon as I would forgive him, he would do the same stuff. I'm not about to go down that road again. Been there done that and got the t-shirt to prove it." Myra responds.

"I hear you, but you know Xavier and Larry are nothing alike. I know Xavier was wrong on all levels, but he definitely is not Larry." I say.

"I hear what you're saying Chas, but I got to be careful and until Xavier proves he can show me some respect, I'm not about to let him all in my face again."

"I agree with you on that. Boys got to know we mean what we say when we want to be respected. That's what I love about my Patrick." Monica shares.

"Okay what's up with you and your soul mate?" Chandra asks.

"Well, that trick, Trena tried to come at me again with her shady comments, but my Patrick stood up for me again and let her know she doesn't have a chance."

"Go Team Patrick!" I say as I give Monica a high-five.

"Yup, that's my boo. He set her straight and let her know that every boy don't want to have sex with her especially him. We walked away from her and left her speechless. We made sure we were all hugged up as we walked away too. I don't think I'm going to hear anything else from her for a while." Monica waves her hand in the air as if she's giving God some praise.

"I'm glad about that because I would hate to see our anointed lead singer in our group swing on that girl for calling you names or for trying to take your boo," Chandra laughs and so do we all. We knew Monica was about to stomp that girl.

"Okay, okay.....you all are real funny. Anyway, what's up with you Chandra? How has Brian been acting lately?"

"He's been trying to give me hints about having sex. He keeps saying we need to do some other things. I was like, I'm not down for that at all. I'm not about to give up those panties to nobody." Chandra says after taking a sip of her chocolate milk.

"You better say that. If he can't respect that, then brother got to go." Monica responds.

"Yeah, I don't know what's up with him, but lately I've seen him talking to Tyrik Smalls and since then his talk has changed. So I got to see what's up. He wants me to go to this party with him so I'll see if he brings it up again."

"Girl, that Tyrik Smalls ain't nothing but trouble. He's really out there. I just wonder how his life is going to end up. I heard he can play basketball real good, but he's so busy doing crazy stuff outside of school that I don't know how he's going to make it." Myra says while she's cutting up her apple.

"Yes, I'm wondering if he's ever going to graduate. I think he stayed back two times already." I respond.

172

"Well, I hope Brian stays away from him because he don't need nobody to stop him from graduating and getting a football scholarship. I'll see how this party goes and see what he's up to."

"That's cool……" I stop my sentence because I see Jonathan and Shayna coming towards our table. Jonathan has this look on his face like he's coming to start some drama. Shayna is walking all close to him like she's his body guard.

"Oh boy….here he comes. Did you set him straight about those pictures yet?" Myra asks me while pushing her tray to the middle of the table.

"No, we didn't get a chance to talk. I only had words with Shayna." I also push my tray to the middle of the table. Not sure how this is going to turn out, but I know I got to face Jonathan. All I know is an apology better come out his mouth before he says anything else.

Chapter 34 – Chastity

"What's up Chas?" Jonathan asks as he wraps his arm around Shayna's shoulders.

"What's up Chas? That's all you got to say to her? You already know what's up." Myra jumps in.

"Ain't nobody talking to you." Shayna chimes in like bodyguards and bullies do.

"And I don't think nobody was talking to you." Chandra says as she stands.

Oh, Lord. Is something about to pop off up in here? I can't let my girls get crazy up in here. The end of the school year is almost over and neither of us needs to get put out of school. Our parents would bust us and First Lady Rice would be so upset to here that her lead singing group was going to miss a concert because we got in a big fight. Jesus take the wheel.

"Alright, let's chill. What do you want Jonathan?" I finally ask.

"I came over here because my girl, Shayna says you and her had a few words about those pictures."

"Yes, we did and what about it?"

"I'm not trying to get you back Chas if that's what you thinking." Jonathan says as Shayna is smiling like she just pulled a string on her puppet.

"Jonathan I never said I wanted to get back with you. I told you already that I just wanted us to be friends. What I want to know is why did you put those pictures in the chat group?"

"Friends? Chas, me and you been together since eighth grade and you just going to push me to the side like that?"

Wait a minute. Where is this going? Doesn't he know Shayna is right next to him? Jesus, please take the wheel. I look at Myra, Monica and Chandra to see their expressions and they look confused just like I do. What is Jonathan talking about?

"Jonathan, what in the world are you talking about? You acted like I was a complete stranger when I thought I was pregnant. You cut me off then, but as soon as you found out I wasn't pregnant then you wanted to be up all in my face. You got it all twisted. I don't want to get back with you. You don't respect me and all you want is what I got down here." I did one of Shayna's moves and patted myself on my private area.

"Now that's truth right there." Chandra chimes in.

"See that's why I posted them pictures because you act like you too good for me now. I told you that if we didn't get back together I was going to do something."

"Hold up. Did you say you was trying to get her back?" Shayna jumps in.

Bingo. Ding, ding, ding. You finally getting it, Shayna. I hope she is beginning to understand what I was trying to tell her earlier. These boys aren't respecting her at all. They just want her for her body.

"Chill, Shayna. Chas was my girl for a long time. I can't help it if she still got a piece of my heart."

"So what you trying to say, Jonathan? I'm your girl now and you getting all this and you still trying to get with this trick." Shayna says as she pushes Jonathan's arm from off her shoulder and folds her arms across her chest.

We all looking at them to see what they're going to do next.

"Shayna, I don't know why you tripping. You already knew what it was. You the rebound girl. Chas didn't want me back so I got with you. I only did that because everybody said you was easy. That's what you rep so I made my move. Chas will always have my heart."

Boom and there it is. I hope Shayna getting this downloaded in her head and her heart. She better stop being so easy.

Shayna said a few curse words and started walking away. Before she could get out of hearing range, I yelled out to her.

"Shayna we're having our session Saturday at twelve noon. Hope you coming."

I turn to look at Jonathan. "Jonathan, I need you to take those pictures off the chat. You don't know all the stuff people are saying about me and people giving me all these strange looks. I can't believe you did that to me."

"Okay, Chas I'll take them down. I'm really sorry. I just got so mad that you wouldn't take me back. I know I messed up, but do you think you would give me another chance?" Jonathan looks like a sad puppy dog who hasn't been fed in a day.

Myra, Monica and Chandra are giving me the side eye. They looking at me right now like they daring me to say yes to Jonathan so they can jump me as soon as I answer.

"Jonathan, I think it's best that we keep it the way it is for now. I'm just not ready to jump into a relationship right now."

"Yeah, but I see you all in the new dude's face."

"He's just new here and needs somebody to talk to. Besides, if I wanted to date somebody else I can do that. You don't own me and plus you've been running around with Shayna."

"I told you, I only got with Shayna to make you mad and because everybody said she was easy."

"That's a shame how you doing that girl, Jonathan. She got feelings too and you know better."

"Whatever, Chas. I'm not worried about her. I want my old girl back that's all I want."

"Well, I'm not ready for nothing like that. So, please take those pictures down and let's just keep it as friends for now."

"Alright Chas I'll take the pictures down, but I'm not giving up on us just yet. I'll back off for a few if that's what you want. I'll see you later." Jonathan says as he leans in and kisses me on my cheek. I let him do it and give him a hug. Even though I have no plans to get back with Jonathan, he still has a place in my heart.

As Jonathan walks away, me, Myra, Monica and Chandra take a deep breath as a sigh of relief. Mission accomplished and we didn't even have to throw no punches.

Chapter 35 – Myra

I'm so glad everything worked out with Chastity and Jonathan. For a minute there I thought we were going to have to set him straight. He is so wrong for what he said about Shayna though. I kind of feel bad for her. I know how it is when a guy just wants to use you. I hope she comes to the session with First Lady Rice. She probably needs to.

As I'm answering the last question on my English homework, I hear my mother calling me from her bedroom.

"Myra, come in my room. I want you to look at something."

I get up and walk into my mother's room. When I look at her I can't believe what I'm seeing, but maybe she thinks she looks good.

Her black dress is so tight it probably is touching the inside of her body. Her breasts are bulging out of the top of the dress and you can see her kitty cat tattoo that sits on her left breast. The dress is so short it reaches to the middle of her thighs with a tie string on the side.

I'm thinking to myself like where is she going dressed like that? I mean she's like over forty and the way she's dressed looks like she's stuck in her twenties.

"How do I look?" My mom asks after I've stared at her for at least five minutes.

I'm not sure how I should answer this question. I want to tell her the truth, but I don't want to hurt her feelings either. She looks a hot mess, but how do you tell your mother she looks like she's a woman ready to walk the streets. Either way I look at it, it's not going to be good.

"Where are you going?" I finally ask.

"I'm going out on a date!" My mother says as she skips a little in her heels.

A date? Really? Like didn't you just deal with a crazy man and then the other man dumped you because you had children. This is too much for me. I understand now why First Lady and Pastor Rice share about women jumping from one relationship to the next. A woman needs time to heal from her relationships is what we hear at church.

"Mom, don't you think your dress is a little tight."

"Tight? Girl, this dress is sexy. You got to understand that don't no man want a woman dressed in a dress that looks like a potato sack." My mother says as she walks around the room turning around and looking at her booty in the mirror.

Dang being over forty got women tripping about how they booty looks in a dress. Well, at least it got my mother tripping. I have no words.

"Mom, who do you have a date with?"

"Myra, he's big time. Bigger than Robert was. He works for the Mayor and is some type of city official. I really don't know what he does actually, but I know the brother got money because he works real close to the Mayor."

Oh boy. Here we go. My mother loves money or at least she loves spending other people's money. I'm glad she's slowed down on the drinking a bit, but every now and then she will slip her a drink. I hope tonight won't be one of those nights because when she drinks she gets a little loud and wild.

"Okay, so where did you meet him?" I ask. I'm not really interested in knowing about him. I'm more concerned about my mom. She really needs a break from these men. I really wish she would just come to church more often.

"Now this is going to sound real strange, but I met him in the grocery store. He was so nice and down to earth. I thought he would be so uppity by how he was dressed, but he was cool. He's not completely my type, but he looks good and he got money." My mother says while she's strapping up her heels.

If I hear her say he got money one more time, I'm going to scream. I wonder is he saved. Does he go to church? I have to laugh at myself because I'm starting to sound like one of the church mothers. Wait, did she say she met him in a grocery store? So was it in the frozen section, the meat department or by the fresh fruits?

"Okay so you gave him your number and he asked you on a date?" I ask.

"Yes! We talked for a few days and then he asked me to go out with him on this special dinner party. So, listen Myra I got to hurry up and finish getting ready because he'll be here soon."

"Okay, but Mom did you tell him you have children?" I ask because I don't want her to have to go through all that drama again that she just went through with this last dude.

"Yes, I made sure I told him I had two children. He has a son of his own too, but he really doesn't see him that much."

"Why not? Does he live in another state?"

"I don't know all the details just yet, but I'll find out. We'll talk about it later when I get home."

"Okay." I walk out of my mother's room with two thoughts on my mind. One, I hope this works out for her this time and if it doesn't, the second thing I hope it does is draw her to God so she can go back to church with me. I guess we'll have to wait and see.

Chapter 36 – Chandra

I'm waiting on Brian to pick me up for this party. He said he would be here about fifteen minutes ago, but I haven't seen him and he hasn't called. That's strange for him because Brian is usually on time for everything. With his dad being in the military for so many years, he makes sure he's on time. So, I guess I'm on the military hurry up and wait status right about now.

I guess I'll take this time to check on my makeup. I walk over to my dresser, look in the mirror and add a little more gold eyeshadow. The color brings out my light brown eyes. I glance at my watch and then my cell phone makes a noise to let me know I have a text.

"Hey Chandra. I'm running late. Do you think you can meet me at the party?

"Can't I just wait for you Brian? I really don't know where I'm going anyway."

"I can give you the address….hold up I'll send it in a few."

I know Brian doesn't think I'm going to roll up to some party on my own that I know nothing about. I thought this was for the football players and their guests. I'm not going by myself. I wonder if Monica will be there with Patrick. I don't remember her saying anything about it, but maybe she plans to surprise me. If Brian thinks I'm driving there, then I guess I won't be going to this party.

"Here's the address – 345 Sterling Ridge Road. I got to pick up something for the party."

"Brian, I'm not going to this party without you. I don't feel right going by myself."

"Chandra, you'll be okay. Nobody is going to bother you. I'll be there. I'm just running late."

"Why can't I just wait for you?" I'm really not feeling this at all. I'm not walking up in there with a bunch of football players and whoever else. Monica and I are the only ones dating football players. I'll just call Monica and see if she'll ride with me.

"Come on Chandra."

"It's cool. I'm going to call Monica and see if I can just ride with her and Patrick." I text back.

Just as I'm about to search my phone for Monica's number, my cell phone rings. It's Brian.

"Hey Chandra. You don't have to call Monica. I'll come get you because I'm not sure if Patrick is coming tonight."

"Oh okay. I know Monica didn't say nothing about it so I was wondering. How much longer will it be?"

"I can come get you in about fifteen minutes, but I still got to pick up these sodas too. I can take you to the party and then go back out and get the sodas." Brian says.

Why does this boy keep trying to drop me off at this party without him? I don't get it. Does he even want me to come tonight?

"Brian, do you want me to go to this party with you or what?" I finally ask. Time to cut to the chase.

"Yeah…..I want you to come."

I hear Brian talking, but for some reason he sounds a little nervous and not at all convincing that he wants me to go to this party.

"Okay, but you sure don't sound like it. I'll be waiting on you when you come. Just text me when you're outside."

"Okay, Chandra. See you in a few."

Fifteen minutes has passed and I hear my phone give me that signal to let me know I have a text. It's Brian. He's finally outside waiting for me.

I look in the mirror one last time and then let my parents know that I'm leaving out. I walk down the driveway and when I get to the car, I jump in and lean over to give Brian a kiss. I notice that he's sweating on his forehead.

"You alright?" I ask.

"Yeah I'm cool. You look pretty."

I blush. "Thank you. You look good too."

We are silent for about ten minutes, which is awkward because we usually talk to one another. We pull up to this house and Brian stops the car.

"Okay, we're here. Just follow me when we get inside. I want you to relax and let's enjoy each other tonight, okay?"

"Okay, Brian. How long are we going to stay?"

"I don't know. Let's see how it is first."

We get out the car and walk up the steps to get to the front door. Brian knocks on the front door and I'm in shock when I see who opens the front door. It definitely was not one of the Midland Central football players. This person would never even be considered for the team. I have absolutely no words to even say. All I can do is look at Brian to see if I could tell whether he knew anything about Tyrik Smalls answering the door to a football team's house party.

"Hey what's up bruh. Glad you finally got here." Tyrik said while dapping up Brian. He had a red solo cup in his hand. I have a funny feeling that it definitely wasn't filled with soda.

"Cool. You remember my girl, Chandra."

"Yeah, the one you ain't got down with......" Tyrik starts, but Brian interrupts him.

"Chill, man. Are you going to let us in or what?"

"Yeah come on in and enjoy yourself." Tyrik tells us before he drinks whatever he has in that red cup.

"Yeah we plan to, right Chandra?" Brian says while looking straight into my eyes.

"As long as I'm with you."

"I got you." Brian says while grabbing my hand to lead us inside the house.

"Yeah, that's what I'm talking about. Grab a little something to eat and make sure you get something to drink." Tyrik adds while we pass by him.

When we get inside there really aren't a lot of people in the house. I didn't see a DJ and the music playing was kind of low and everybody seemed to be into their own thing. Nobody was dancing. What kind of celebration party for the football players was this? As a matter of fact I don't really see any of the football players that I'm familiar with.

"They look like they're really just getting started. Let's grab a little something to eat and get something to drink." Brian whispers to me in my ear.

"Okay, I'm following you, but I don't really see any of the players here." I whisper back.

"I guess they're running late like we were." Brian responds while pulling me towards the table with the food and drinks. I grab a hotdog and chips and a soda. Nothing else looks good.

"Hey, Brian you two can go in that room down the hall and chill."

"Alright man, thanks." Brian says as he and I walk down the hallway.

I'm not so sure I want to go in a room in a house I'm not familiar with, but I told Brian I would come tonight and follow him.

"Brian, do you think they have any ice? You know I like ice in my soda and the way that this soda can feels I can tell it's really not that cold." I say as we walk into what looks like a guest room.

"Okay, I'll see if they got another cold soda and get you some ice for it." Brian says.

Before I answer him completely, he is already out the door. He sure is acting a little strange. Every answer he gives is so short, he hasn't been saying too much, he's sweating a bit more than usual and we're at Tyrik Smalls' house. Why in the world are we here at his house? Why is he throwing a party for the football players?

Brian returns just as fast as he left. "Here's your soda Chandra. I poured it in the cup for you and put some ice in it. It should be cold now. Let's eat this food and chill for a bit. I guess they'll start playing some real music soon."

"Okay, thanks Brian." I take the soda and drink some of it before I start eating my hot dog.

After I bite some of the hot dog, I notice Brian just staring at me like he's seen a ghost.

"Are you okay, Brian?"

"Yeah, I'm good. You look real pretty tonight."

"Thank you. You look good too."

"I know I'm going to get me a kiss tonight, right?" Brian asks after he drinks some of his soda.

I eat a few chips and drink some more of my soda before answering him.

"Yeah, you might get a little something, something." I laugh and so does Brian.

We keep talking and then all of a sudden I start feeling a little drowsy and the room doesn't look as clear. I could tell Brian was looking at me, but he wasn't saying anything or at least I didn't think he was.

"You good, Chandra?" Brian finally asks.

"I feel kind of funny like I'm going to pass out or something."

I notice Brian coming closer to me and then I hear a door open. The voice says, "Bruh is she out yet? You better get that."

"Yo, be quiet. I got to run to the bathroom real quick. Where is it?" Brian asks.

"The bathroom up here is broken so you have to go downstairs to the bathroom which is right near the kitchen."

"Okay, I'll be right back. Make sure she's okay until I get back, Tyrik."

"Oh yeah, I'll make sure she's good."

I can barely make out what Brian was saying because as each minute passes it feels like I'm getting ready to black out. I see this other person coming towards me. By now, I'm lying on the bed because I can barely sit up. I'm able to notice that it's Tyrik coming close to me.

He leans in closer to me and says, "You been holding back on my boy, but you about to give it up now. He's going to get it and I'm going to get it too." Tyrik laughs.

I'm really fading out and can't really talk clearly, but I can feel Tyrik unbuttoning my blouse.

"Whaaattttt aaaarrrreee yooooou doinnnnnnnnng?" I managed to slur the words out of my mouth. I really don't understand why I can't talk right. Everything was coming together.

My blouse is off and I hear Tyrik say, "You giving it up tonight."

After he says that I can feel him trying to remove my skirt. I'm drifting quickly. I feel him climb on top of me. I can't fight him. I have no strength. I can barely understand what's happening, but in the back of my mind I'm wondering where is Brian. What was taking him so long? Did he just leave me here with Tyrik?

Chapter 37 — Chandra

"Chandra, Chandra are you okay? Please tell me you can hear me. I'm so sorry Chandra. I'm so sorry."

I can barely hear the voice speaking to me, but I know it sounds like Brian.

"I should have never took you to Tyrik's house. I can't believe he tripped me up like that. I can't believe I even fell for it all. I didn't mean for this to happen to you Chandra."

I hear what Brian is saying, but I'm not really understanding why he's saying what he's saying.

"Chandra, can you hear me? Are you okay?" Brian says as he shakes my body a little. From what I can tell, I'm sitting in his car.

"Yes, I hear you. What happened?" I respond very slowly.

"Chandra, I hate to even tell you. I'm so sorry. I hope you forgive me."

"Brian, tell me what happened. I remember Tyrik taking my blouse off and then he…." I stop there because for some reason it's taking me a minute to clearly understand what happened. The dizziness is slowly going away.

"Yes, that dude tried to rape you. When I came back from using the bathroom and walked into the room, I saw him climbing on top of you. I couldn't believe it. I just snapped and started punching him until he fell on the bedroom floor." Brian says while he's rubbing my forehead with a wet rag.

I sit up a little more in my seat after hearing what Brian just said. I'm trying to understand if I really heard what he said.

"Rape me? Are you serious? Why would he do that?"

"Yes, I'm serious. Tyrik is no good just like you always tried to tell me. I don't even know why I was following him up."

"Brian, I don't understand this at all. I know I'm still a little dizzy, but I'm trying to figure out why I'm feeling this way and why I blacked out for a while."

Brian stares at me for what seems like a long time. I tap him on the shoulder to see if he's okay. He looks into my eyes deeply. It's almost scary.

"Chandra, you got to promise me you will forgive me for what I'm about to tell you."

"What are you talking about Brian?" Here we go with the riddles again. I don't understand why boys take so long to say what they have to say. Maybe because they're trying to come up with a good believable lie. I don't know, but with the way I'm feeling I wish Brian would just come out with it.

"Chandra, I know you kept wondering why I was talking to Tyrik. Well, he kept coming up to me wanting to know had we did the nasty. When I kept telling him no not yet, he kept pushing me to get with you. That's why I started telling you we need to do more than just kiss, but I really didn't mean for this to happen Chandra. You got to believe me. I know I was wrong, but I didn't want that to happen to you." Brian says and then turns his head to look out the window of the car. He then punches the steering wheel.

"Brian, what else? I mean how come I'm feeling so dizzy?" I ask.

"Tyrik said he had something to give to me to put in your drink so you would pass out and I could have sex with you."

"So it just wasn't Tyrik who was thinking about raping me, but you was about to try to take it without my consent too!" I yell as I punch Brian in the arm.

"Chandra, I'm sorry. I wasn't thinking straight. I just got tired of him asking and teasing me about it and then he started telling the other players that I hadn't did nothing with you yet. So I gave into the pressure and asked you to come to his place."

"I can't believe you, Brian. I thought you were different. I thought you and I had a good thing going and you understood why I didn't want to have sex."

"It's good with us Chandra. I just…..well I'm human. I'm really into you, Chandra and I would be lying if I said I didn't want to have sex with you. I want you to forgive me and I'll back up from asking you about that because I really do respect."

"Did he rape me?" I ask while a tear was streaming down my cheek.

Brian wipes my face. "No! I saw him climbing on top of you and then I jumped him and started punching on him. He didn't have his pants off and you still had your underwear on. Chandra, I'm so sorry. Will you forgive me?"

"I know I have to forgive you because I'm a Christian, but I don't know if we should still see each other."

"Chandra, don't say that…..I mean I know I messed up, but I don't want us to end like this. Let me make it up to you. I promise nothing like this will ever happen again."

"Yeah, I know it won't happen again because we're not going to be seeing each other like that. I can't be with someone who doesn't respect me."

"I get it, but don't answer tonight. Let me get you home and let's talk about it tomorrow or even later this week." Brian pleads.

"Okay Brian." I didn't want to say anymore because I partly already knew what I was going to do. I like Brian so much, but I can't be with someone who would stoop that low to have sex with me without my consent.

I know he felt the pressure from his peers, but I can't help, but wonder what would have happened if Tyrik didn't do what he did and Brian followed through with the original plan. Don't they call this kind of stuff date rape? Who's to say he won't try it again? I can't be a statistic…..I can't.

Chapter 38 – Myra

My mother is out on a dinner date with the same guy she says she met at the grocery store. He's still a mystery man to me because neither Michael nor I have met him yet. I have no clue about this man, but I do know she at least told him that she had children. She mentioned something about him having a son, but that's about all I know. Oh yeah, she said he had money, which seems to be on the top of her list when it comes to dating someone.

After all she and I have been through with these guys, I don't see how she does it. I'm still tripping over what Xavier said. Not sure if I'm going to give him another chance or not. The other day, he dropped off a dozen roses for me at the house. I wasn't home, but my brother got them for me and put them in a vase and placed them on the kitchen table. They are beautiful. No one has ever given me a dozen roses before. Xavier is really nice and I'm sure he just let his raging hormones get the best of him, but I'm not so sure I'm ready for all this. I probably need to chill myself.

I finish up with doing my homework so I think I'm going to the living room and look at some television. I have no idea what's on tonight, so I guess I'll just be flicking the channels until I find something. My mind needs a break from working all those calculus problems.

I take a seat in the recliner chair; the most comfortable seat in the living room. As I'm flicking through these channels, I hear this loud noise outside. It sounds like two people are arguing. I get quiet to listen more and I can tell that it's a man and a woman. The voices are getting louder so I get up and peek outside the window to see who it is. This kind of noise doesn't usually happen in our neighborhood.

When I look out the window, I notice this man slapping this woman. He's arguing with her and she's yelling at him. I look a little closer and realize it's my mother.

I run to the door, open it and scream, "Ma!"

The man gets into his car and takes off. I run to the end of the driveway where my mother is and I grab her around her waist.

"Ma, who is that? Why did he slap you?"

My mother starts crying and begins to talk through all the sobbing, "I don't know. He was about to come in the house to meet you and Michael and we started talking about his ex-wife and their son. All of a sudden it's like he snapped when I said it didn't make sense to me that he doesn't go visit his son. I told him he must have done something really bad for his ex-wife not to want him to be around her or his son. He started arguing and slapped me."

"That is crazy! That's probably why he's not around them. He probably was slapping her around too. Are you okay, Ma?"

"Yes, I'm okay, but I can't stand all these bad relationships. I'm sick of it. Nobody seems to want me."

"Ma, don't worry about that. A good man will come your way the minute you stop looking. I wish you would come to church with me. First Lady Rice always says to let God handle what we know we can't."

"I don't want to hear all that now, Myra. I want to have someone special in my life." My mother yells back while holding her face.

"You got me and Michael. We love you." I say as we continue to walk back into the house.

"Myra, you know I'm not talking about you and Michael. I want someone that I can live happily ever after with. I don't want to grow old alone."

"Ma, it's going to be okay." I say as I rub her back.

"There is no need for me to be here. You and Michael can do better by yourselves. You don't need me." My mother says as she walks quickly into her bedroom.

I walk after her, "Ma, what are you talking about?"

She slams the door in my face. I stand outside for a while until I start hearing her yell that she's not good enough and nobody wants her and she'd be better off not here. I call out to her, but she does not answer. I'm pacing the floor and I let ten minutes go by and call out to her again. Still no answer. I can't take this anymore. I finally open the door and I see my mother gulping down something and drinking water after it.

I run to her side and notice that she had taken the rest of her pain medication that she had for her back pain. I know there were at least twenty pills in there. I only saw five in the jar.

"Ma, what are you trying to do to yourself?" I say as I shake her.

"Myra, you don't need me. Nobody wants me." My mother says as she lays across her bed.

I call out her name several times and then I realize that I had better call 9-1-1. I run back into the living room to get my phone.

"What's going on?" Michael asks as he sees me running to the living room.

"Mom just took a bunch of pills I got to call the ambulance." I say as fast as I can while I go get my cell phone to make the call.

"What!!! No way. Ma!" Michael yells as he runs to our mother's bedroom. I can hear him calling out for my mother to wake up and he's telling her that he loves her. This is so sad.

I know my mother and I didn't see eye-to-eye about everything; especially about her dating these men, but not having her around was not what I wanted to happen. I know she was feeling lonely, but I didn't know it was at this level.

This ambulance better come quick because I cannot lose my mother because of a man.

Chapter 39 — Myra

"Ma, how are you feeling now?" I ask as I place the hot cup of tea on the table next to my mother's bed.

"I'm doing much better now. I really want to thank you Myra for saving my life."

My mother had my brother and I scared the other day when she took those pills. When she arrived at the hospital, they were able to pump her stomach and they released her shortly after that.

She kept saying she was feeling overly depressed about being single for so long. I really can't understand her pain because after all she's been through with certain men, she ought to be glad she's single. From what I hear from some of the single women in the church, they are pretty much content with it. Of course, I know they want to be married, but they don't go around threatening to take their lives or start popping pills. My mom needs the Lord way down deep in her heart.

"Ma, I love you. I know sometimes I give you a hard way to go, but I don't want to lose you. You really scared me and Michael."

"I really didn't mean to. I don't know what came over me. I guess I was fed up with all these crazy men I keep attracting. I started feeling like something was wrong with me." My mother says as she grabs the cup of tea from off the table. She takes a few sips of it.

"Ma, I know I keep saying the same thing to you, but I really wish you would come to church with me. You would feel a whole lot better and maybe you can allow God to fill that emptiness instead of trying to let a man fill that space."

"Myra, how did you become so smart about relationships?" My mother laughs a little.

"From church. We have such good sessions with First Lady Rice and Pastor Rice always talks about how people need to heal first before jumping into a relationship. He always says to let God have you first."

"It sounds like you really be listening."

"Yeah, it took a minute because when I was with Larry I wasn't even trying to hear all that at first. Then when all that drama started happening with him and Mr. Leroy, I really started to pay attention. That's why I keep asking you to come to church."

"Myra, I think I may just take you up on that. I tried everything else; maybe I can give God a try too."

"Yes!!! You won't regret it. We got a concert coming up so I know you will enjoy that too."

I hug my mother and then I leave out of her room so she can get some more rest to gain her strength back. I'm so glad she's finally going to come to church again. I hope this time it will be for keeps.

Chapter 40 – Chastity

"Girls, let's settle down a bit so we can get started with our session. We have quite a few things to cover so I wanted to begin in about five minutes. If you have to use the restroom, please do it now so we don't have a lot of people walking out when we have our discussion." First Lady Rice says as she walks around the room making sure everyone gets in their places.

We usually have these quarterly sessions with First Lady Rice to discuss different things. We get a chance to share what's going on with us and get feedback from the group and from her. Then after we finish our discussion, we get to eat. Everybody likes that part because the food is so good.

I'm at the sink in the kitchen finishing up with washing my hands and when I turn around I see Myra coming in the door.

"Hey, Myra. How is your mom?" I say as I give her a hug.

"Hey. She's doing better. She really had Michael and I really scared. I thought we were going to lose her."

"Wow. That is scary. I don't know if I would be able to handle my mom doing that either. I'm glad she's better."

"Yeah, me too. She's coming to church tomorrow. She said she tried everything else, she might as well try God."

"Okay then! That's good to hear. At least she's coming and hopefully she'll come to the concert too." I add.

"Yes, she'll be there." Myra responds as she waves at Monica and Chandra coming in the door.

"Hey, what's up?" Monica asks.

"Nothing much. Getting ready for this session. I hope my guest shows up, but with her it's no telling." I share as I give a hug to Monica and Chandra.

"What guest? Who did you invite?" Chandra asks.

"Shayna Jefferson." I say while clasping my hands together.

Myra tilts her head to the side and says, "Girl, you got to be kidding me."

I laugh at Myra. "I don't know what came over me, but when she started popping off at the mouth about Jonathan, the sweet Christian girl in me started inviting her to church. She need help ya'll."

The girls laugh at me as we walk towards our table.

"You a good one because I know ain't no way I'm inviting Trena Lewis to this session. I'm just saying. I'm keeping it real. I need to go to the altar a few more times on that." Monica says as she takes her seat at the table.

"Girl, you are a trip!" Myra says.

"No, girl I'm a journey! I'm keeping it one hundred." Monica responds.

"Ya'll need to quit. Hopefully she'll come because I think she needs some help. She thinks every boy wants her panties. It's crazy." I whisper.

"Sometimes those boys do just want the panties and they will do whatever they can think of to get them by any means necessary." Chandra says as she rolls her eyes.

"Awww, Chandra I can't even imagine what you went through with Brian and that crazy Tyrik. He is nothing but trouble, but I'm really can't believe Brian fell for all that." I say.

"I know that is terrible, Chandra. Were you able to press charges?" Myra asks.

"We tried, but because he really didn't rape me they said I really didn't have a case. All I could do is put a restraining order on him."

I place my hand on Chandra's shoulder. "That's crazy. So what about Brian? Have you decided what you're going to do?"

"No, I haven't really decided yet. I'm not talking to him though. I just don't think I can trust him again. He sent me a teddy bear and candy to apologize again, but I haven't even told him thank you." Chandra shares.

Our conversation is interrupted when First Lady Rice tells everyone to listen up because she's about to begin the first session.

"Okay, girls let's go ahead and get started with our first session. You know we have a lot to discuss so we're going to begin with the first hot topic and that is our sex talk and how it can create a lot of stress for you teen girls. It has so much stress attached to it at your age that it's best to remain abstinent. The first stressor that comes with having sex is that you may get pregnant. Some of you know some teen girls who have had babies this year. I'm sure many of them are going through stress because they are not only responsible for themselves, but they are responsible for another human being for the rest of their lives. Sometimes this choice blocks them from finishing school or going off to college."

I raise my hand to make a comment.

"Yes, Chastity. Do you have question or point you would like to make?" First Lady Rice asks.

"Yes ma'am. I remember last year when I thought I was pregnant, I was so stressed out because of it. I was so glad to find out that I wasn't pregnant. Since then I've been abstinent."

"I'm glad to hear that you are still living a life of abstinence. Girls, it's better to just wait until you get married."

Monica raises her hand. "I got a question First Lady Rice."

"Okay, Monica go ahead with your question and then we'll move on to the next topic." First Lady Rice says while grabbing her glass of water.

"What is it with all these females that keep giving it up? I mean they think every boy wants to have sex with them and they're always chasing after some boy. Something ain't right." Monica says while shaking her head.

"I agree with you on that Monica. I don't get it. Why do these girls keep doing that?" I ask.

"Well, girls first of all, that is a good question. I'm sure there are many reasons as to why some girls tend to behave this way, but I'll share a couple of them. Many times, teen girls don't understand their value. They don't recognize their self-worth. Many girls don't love themselves because they've never been taught to. You girls have to realize that you are fearfully and wonderfully made by the hands of God. You are beautiful in His sight. You girls must love who you are right now. Don't worry about the mistakes you made because those can be forgiven, but it's so important to know that you are good enough. Your life is significant and loving yourself first is important if you want to have healthy relationships in the future. The other reason could be that the person experienced sexual assault or molestation. It is so unfortunate, but some girls go through sexual abuse or molestation at some point in their lives. If they have not totally healed from those attacks, then they could be trying to soothe their pain through sex. Some people who have experienced this kind of trauma in their lives may do things they wouldn't normally do because of what happened."

Somebody raises their hand in the back because I notice First Lady Rice directing her eyes towards the back of the room.

"Do you have a question young lady? Tell us your name also." First Lady Rice asks while pointing her finger to the back.

I didn't turn around to see who it was until the girl says her name.

"My name is Shayna Jefferson. I went through that." She says and then drops her head slightly.

First Lady Rice pauses for a minute to wait for her to continue, but she doesn't.

"You went through what, Shayna? Do you want to share what you mean? It's okay to share now or we can talk after this session." First Lady Rice says as she walks a little closer to where Shayna is.

"I was molested three times and it still bothers me so much. The person was a close friend of the family. My grandmother did take me to talk to someone about it, but it still hurts. The counselor said the same thing about when I let boys have sex with me it's a way to sooth the pain. I know it sounds crazy, but I just got wild after all that happened. I really want to change." Shayna says as she starts to cry.

I grab some tissues out of my purse and walk over to where Shayna was sitting. Who would have thought in a million years that I would be bringing a tissue to Shayna Jefferson? Sometimes you just never know what people are going through. We just see the outward, but we never know what happened to make them that way. I feel sorry for her, but now I understand.

I hand the tissue to Shayna and then First Lady Rice gives her a hug.

First Lady Rice turns to me. "Did you invite her, Chastity?"

"Yes ma'am. I didn't know she went through that." I reach over and give Shayna hug too. Shortly, after I hug Shayna, a few other girls come to hug Shayna too.

Everyone hugs Shayna and we calm her down. First Lady Rice walks back to the front of the room and continues to share.

"Well, young ladies as you can see you never know what someone else has gone through. There is a reason why people act the way that they do. I'm glad you felt comfortable to open up and share Shayna. You are more than welcome to keep coming to our sessions. I think it will really help you. I would love to talk with you after this session."

"Yes, ma'am I would like that." Shayna says.

"Great! Okay, young ladies let's go over one last topic about relationships. What have been some of your experiences this year when it comes to having relationships with boys? What are some things you've learned? What are some things you will never do again?" First Lady Rice says as she looks around the room to see who will speak first.

Chandra raises her hand.

"Go ahead Chandra. What would you like to share about relationships?"

"Well, I didn't necessarily go through what Shayna went through, but it was kind of close. Some of you probably already heard that I've been dating Brian Miller for a couple of months. Well, he started asking me to have sex, but I would tell him no and that I was waiting until I get married. I guess he got tired of hearing that so he invited me to this party and someone talked him into putting something in my soda so that I would pass out." Chandra takes a deep breath and grabs a tissue from the box in the center of the table.

"Take your time Chandra." First Lady Rice says while walking closer to our table. She places her hand on Chandra's shoulder.

Chandra continues, "So Brian leaves the room to use the bathroom and I continue to eat my food and drink the soda. I started feeling out of it to the point that I didn't even know what was going on around me. Then this dude, who I will not name at this time, came in the room and started to take my clothes off. He was able to take my shirt off and then he started to take my skirt off and he climbed on top of me. By then, Brian walked back in the room and started beating up on this boy. So what I have to say about the whole thing is I'm not dating anybody that wants to just have sex with me and who will disrespect me as a female."

"Chandra I appreciate you sharing that experience and I'm so sorry that you had to go through it. You girls really have to be careful who you allow in your life. No one should disrespect you or take advantage of you at all. You have purpose and destiny over your lives and you don't have time to waste it with someone who really doesn't care about you. As Chandra has shared her story, I must warn you about date rape drugs. There are drugs out there that people can put in your drink and cause you to do things that you have no control over. If you're at a party with a crowd of people and you walk away from something you're drinking, which I hope is just soda, I wouldn't drink it. Be careful girls."

Myra's hand goes up. "First Lady Rice, thank you for sharing about all of this with us. I know the talk you gave us before about relationships and respecting ourselves really helped me get through my situation with Larry."

"You are so welcome, Myra. That's what I'm here for; to help you girls out."

"I want to ask if you could pray for my mother. She got depressed about dating the wrong men. Some of you remember the issue we had with Mr. Leroy. Well, since then she's been dating on and off and all of them were crazy. She got fed up and took some pills. She's okay now, but I want us to pray for her. She said she was coming to church tomorrow."

"Okay, Myra. We can definitely do that. I'm glad that you're mom is doing better and I'm glad she'll be coming to church."

First Lady Rice walks back towards the front of the room where she has her notes.

"Well, young ladies we have ran out of time, but I hope that something that was shared today will help you to understand how important it is to love yourself, respect yourself and demand respect from others by how you carry yourself. Oh, and remember to respect others because you never know what they are going through. Let's gather in a circle and have our closing prayer and we will also lift up Myra's mom in prayer as well."

"And me too. Pray for me too." Shayna says loudly and then she slowly lowers her head.

"Yes, we will pray for you too, Shayna. Thank you for coming and please don't be a stranger. Thank you for inviting her Chastity."

"Yes ma'am."

"Yeah, thanks for inviting me Chastity." Shayna says.

"No problem." I smile at her. It wasn't a fake smile, but a real one because after all she's been through she needs someone to show they care.

Monica whispers to me. "I *got to do better*. Maybe I'll invite Trena Lewis after all…..she may have had the same issue."

"Maybe…..you never know. We are our sister's keeper."

We all grab hands, bow our heads and First Lady leads us into prayer.

Chapter 41 – Myra

"Today is a powerful day because this is the day that the Lord has made and we shall rejoice and be glad in it." Pastor Rice starts his morning service with always telling us that it's a powerful day.

I must agree that it is a powerful day because I'm so glad that my mother has finally made it to church service. She was so excited about coming to church this morning. She shocked Michael and I when we saw that she was dressed and ready before us. She made breakfast for us and everything. Yes, today was a powerful day as Pastor Rice says.

"Can I get a witness in the house?" Pastor Rice continues.

"Amen, Pastor! Preach it." Someone from the congregation yells out.

"You see church, God has some great things in store for your life. Sometimes the enemy wants us to believe that God is not with us, but God is right there waiting for you to allow Him to have full control of your life. Say amen." Pastor Rice shares.

"Amen, Reverend! Say it."

"All He wants is for you to say yes to Him. So many times we put things, possessions and people before God, but we fail to realize that we need God to make it in this life. We got to do better, Saints. We *got to do better*."

"That's the truth!" Someone yells from the back of the church.

"God wants you. He's always wanted you, but He's not going to force Himself on you. He wants you to accept Him. So don't keep running away from Him; run to God."

"Yes Sir! Preach Pastor Rice."

"With that being said, do I have anyone that wants to run to God? Do I have anyone in the congregation that wants to accept Him as Lord and Savior?" Pastor Rice says as he walks slowly down from the pulpit.

My mother nudges me with her elbow. "I'm going up there. I got to get my life together so I'm going to try God this time." My mother whispers.

"You want me to go with you?"

"Sure, that would be good." My mother says as a tear falls slowly down from her eye.

We get up and I start crying a little too. We walk to the altar and my mother gives her life to the Lord. I'm wiping my tears while hugging my mother. As I hug her, I see another person coming down the aisle. Chastity is walking down the aisle with Shayna Jefferson. Imagine that, Shayna Jefferson is giving her life to the Lord. God is amazing.

"I told you today was going to be a powerful day. We have two souls giving their lives to the Lord. Thank you Jesus! It's time for some good singing. Come on Myra, Monica, Chastity and Chandra and use those anointed voices to takes us to worship." Pastor Rice says as he walks back to the pulpit.

We walk to the microphones and use our voices to the glory of God. Even though we might have gone through some things this year, we know that God got us. Today is a powerful day and I got a feeling things are going to get better than ever.